Subjective Serendipity

Christopher Besonen

Published by Besonen Horror, 2022.

For anyone who has ever been at the end of a senseless tragedy
and wondered of the why. Here is my take…

Copyright

This is a work of fiction. Names, places, characters, businesses, places, events or incidents are written in a fictitious manner, or an output of the author's imagination. Any resemblance to any actual persons, living or dead, or actual events, is purely coincidental.

All text contained within this book, rather digital or physical, is protected by copyright law. ©2021-2022. All rights reserved unto Christopher Daniel Besonen, the author, courtesy of the Besonen Horror trademark. No unlicensed reproductions of this book may be used, without written consent by Mr. Besonen.

Prologue:

In the beginning God created the Heaven and the Earth.
For six days, He worked. On the seventh, He rested.

The third planet sat three scores beyond the sun. It was a water world initially, then came the lands, formations of mud, rock and minerals. Like the universe around the third, blackness reigned. A pall sat across the surface of the fiery star in the center of everything. Eternal beings shuffled in the shadowy blank space. Other planets were formed, each one further from the light than the next.

A figure of light, who is revered as God The Maker, was the mightiest of the abiding lurkers. He was to be feared. His wrath, merciless and unmatched. To equal His brutality, the others gave the Earth a multitude of depth, contributing to the Almighty's design.

The ocean reflected its inner self, modeling darkness into an entity. The resulting spirit, wore a sideways crown of embedded blades, an upper body of varying gun blasts, and thighs ragged at the kneecaps, no forelegs. The demon established two realms of his own. The sea born demon built a basement, waiting for the day of his emergence. His patience lasted through centuries of revolutionary growth, before the one he sought was finally born. When she became an adult, in accordance to Earth standards, he shifted into the ideal of her perfect man. His facial features remained, but he was the lord of the manipulative. His seduction was flawless, like his projected looks.

Before the unity of sea demon and woman, long predating it, the dimensions were a blend of the maniacal. Their mashup shared the quality of bloodshed. Thus was coined, 'battle.'

Grand scaled wars were raged using colossal forces. It was then that natural disasters were born, as were the Miscreations. The latter, were

God's defense. His monstrosities, versus the adversary's abominations! God tried three times to renew the grisly game, but His creations were rushed, not in His image. They were slaughtered by The Aboriginables, effortlessly.

The Aboriginables were the metals of Earth, pieced together for massacre. Myths put the responsibility for the expunging of the Miscreated in their mechanized propellerish hands, telling of how they diced the mismatched experiments. The Aboriginables were kin to the vast oceanic waters and the prowling eternals.

God created Hell for the first demon that was loosed, retaliating against the depths of the sea. He numbered the days of The Aboriginables, letting them wallow in their pride for a season. Something that would reflect in End Times. The Aboriginables held the power for a few decades. During this time, when it would rain they bled rust, a sign of the demonic elite.

On that seventh day, God ascended to His Kingdom, spectating from an Utopian view. One particle remained of the Heavenly Father on Earth, meant to taint His good nature. The element of blood thirst. The residue of vengeance was all the lurking ones let show, of the Protagonist that now walked on bars of gold. He decided that when the span of current affairs closed, He would mold a version of mankind in His image. They could be the perfect beings, per the manifestation of rebellion's obstacle not materialize to intervene. History is repetitive, it has always been, surely some menace would arise. Challenging the higher power almost seemed inevitable. All things reflect.

God's cell of retribution remained, leading to the age old question; in the realm of the flesh, is the possibility of peace obtainable?

Chapter 1:
The Stakes Are Raised

The day a state capital burst into flames, Ian knew that his twin brother, Ethan, was the person responsible.

"I see you, same timer," Ian chuckled to himself, cleaning the barrel of his sniper rifle.

When the barrel was spotless, he got on his exercise bike, like he always did when he was stressed about his brother having the upper hand.

"Thirty seven dead politicians, the ante is high," he muttered to himself, his legs burning miles but going nowhere.

"I'll consult the paper," was the final out loud thought from him as he continued to marathon in place.

"Consider the stakes raised," Ethan toasted, raising an alcoholic tea to the news broadcast of his work.

They were born in competition, they would die competing. Ian was born dead. Ethan was delivered in pieces, but alive. Some would say that the manner of their births made each choose their own path of massacre.

"Time for cartoons," Ethan spoke to himself, turning the TV channel away from his biggest blast to date.

Others would say it was their hobbies that embarked them on their missions for death tolls.

Ian chewed on his nicotine gum. His legs wobbly blurs of speed. There was no going back now, only forward. He loved his brother dearly, but the need to be better was infinitely a greater gravity.

Leaping from the bike, he sat down at his typewriter. His primary job was reporter for Circadian Bulletin. With a new gift from his brother making headlines almost daily, the right to gloat was quickly being handed to Ethan. He wrote the details out about the deadly attack, going through a row of gum. He reported from intuition purely when it came to his sibling's work. They had a connection but they weren't telepathic, at least not with one another.

Ethan pictured his brother chewing his teeth down to his gums, fingers clicking across his typewriter, then cackled.

He wrote to his pen pal, a girl he knew a long time ago. They had kept in touch, but she was too involved with her own hobbies for them to make it last. As was Ethan, the game was ever evolving.

'Dearest Cassandra,

I'm sure you've heard about the capital. It reminded me of the time we set the school dumpster on fire. I remember your expression when we realized it was full of cooking oil and how fast it went up. Seems like yesterday, though the years tell me otherwise. Crazy that they have never been able to stop the bombings, isn't it? I wonder if they ever will?

Anyways, how are your days training for space? There's a lot of rumors of a coming visitation. I know you cannot write out if that is factual or not, but could you give an old friend a hint?

Ian sends his love, as always. Hope to hear back soon!

Yours always,

Ethan.'

Ethan sat the pencils down, then cracked his knuckles. He returned his gaze back to toons that act looney, breaking it away just long enough to put the letter into the envelope. It took two episodes of a coyote failing with TNT, before he licked it shut. Another episode, before he put the addresses on the front.

"There it is. A twofer," Ian exclaimed, reading about the man coming in from Hong Kong to receive the rare brain transplant.

Tapping the print button, he memorized the when and where of the procedure, then loaded the rifle.

When he wasn't writing about his twin's body counts, he was typing up articles about his own. The man coming in from the East guaranteed a headliner. He mapped out the how, then kissed the printout.

"Ian, you are an architect," he said aloud, pride filled.

The key to getting away was to keep moving. Nobody knew where the twins would strike, nobody even knew the twins were responsible for the ongoing mayhem. The competition originated between only them, they kept their circle small so that their game wouldn't end prematurely.

Stacy Huff turned the knob on the oven to preheat. If she couldn't have the guy of her dreams then life was simply unfair and not worth living. She looked at herself in the mirror and cursed her existence. If her boyfriend wanted Hannah over her, then she was checking out.

"Selfish prick," she snarled, watching the inside of the stove turn orange with heat.

She petted her cat, Pookins, on his head, feeling him purr as she scratched behind his ears.

"You're the only guy who ever understood me," she told her feline, opening the oven door which blasted her with hot air.

Pookins meowed, his tail raising into the air, as he rubbed up against her.

"So long, bitterness. Farewell, selfish guys with their minds behind the zipper of their pants."

She bent down and kissed her pet, then placed her head into the 450 degrees tomb which had turned red. She blew out the pilot light, and let the carbon monoxide stick to her blood cells.

After feeling nauseous, Stacy passed out. Pookins rubbed against her dead body, waiting for his owner to wake up.

Randy Fouch listened to the new Stef Williams album, not a care in the world. He hummed along, learning the melodies of the songs. Her music was timeless.

His mom drove erratically. She couldn't afford another write up for being late to the job. She blew the horn, weaving in and out of the rush hour jam.

"Knock off that noise," she demanded, not realizing her voice was drowned out by the volume level of the walkman.

She sped past two semi trucks, heading towards the bustling city. One of them honked at her driving, to which she responded with her middle finger. She put her window down, intending to cuss the honking driver out, when the car in front of her came to an abrupt stop. She shrieked, slamming on her brakes. It was too late. The steering wheel embedded into her chest, crushing her heart in the process.

The first semi swerved, clipping the back end of the car. The second didn't have time and instead of hitting the brake, accidentally pressed the gas, flooring into the car's rear where Randy was sitting.

Randy, who was attempting to get his seatbelt off, was pinned. The seatbelt wrapped around his throat.

The driver jumped from his semi, trying to render help, but he couldn't get through the mangled up metal. Beneath it, he could hear the muffled screams of a young boy. He would wake up almost nightly to those haunting tones.

By time the ambulance arrived, Randy was asphyxiated. His mother, dead by the impact of impalement. They were pronounced dead, redirecting traffic down to one lane.

Ian took a detour, cutting past the one lane of traffic ahead.

"I have work to do," he grinned, checking his watch to ensure he was making good time.

With time to spare, he drove to the building across from the Klyne County Medical Center.

"Double caramel latte," he ordered from the cafeteria of the hospital.

Overly sweet drink in his hand, he crossed the one way street, heading back to where his vehicle was parked. He opened the trunk, removing his duffel bag.

Dressed in his best suit, he got on the elevator with the other businessmen, not pressing any buttons.

The small janitor room was conveniently located adjacent from the surgery room. Taking a sip, careful not to place his lips on the cup, Ian put on his gloves and lined up the shot with his fingers.

Through the window to the operating room in the parallel building, he could see the surgeon prepping, as the sound of a helicopter echoed off the skyscrapers of the downtown area.

"You have one shot," he stated to himself, but also speaking to the surgeon who was about to perform the transplant of his career.

Ian watched as the Hong Kong leader was rushed into the room. The surgeon placed a cooler onto the table beside the patient.

"May all that is just and fair, guide my hands," he was saying to his staff, according to reading of his lips from Ian's scope.

Ian chewed on a piece of gum, awaiting the precise moment. The surgeon looked his direction, but the window to the janitor closet was tiny and only the barrel was in view. Only if you were really seeking it would it be noticed.

The surgeon cut off the top of the foreign director's skull, removing the tumor ridden brain. Ian could see his mouth instructing the assisting nurses as the mask over his mouth moved.

When the surgeon presented the new brain, two bullets were fired. The first, burst through the Hong Kong director's head. The second, blew apart the surgeon's scalp.

By the time the hospital staff realized what had happened, Ian was already making his way down the emergency fire stairwell. He changed his clothes, hid his duffel bag away, then drove past the rushing lights of law enforcement.

Police quickly blocked off the surrounding block, searching everyone who came and went from the buildings parallel to the Medical Center.

"Press for the Circadian," Ian introduced, showing his press tag while drinking his latte.

"You guys got here quick."

"Right place, right time. A journalist's curse."

"Just stay out of the way of the investigation," Officer Davis directed, allowing Ian to slip under the crime scene tape.

Ian wrote the notes for his scoop, then left the hospital, just as they were wheeling out the deceased.

"Life is full of tragedy, ain't it?"

"Unjustly so," Ian replied to Officer Davis, who again let him slide underneath the yellow barrier.

Ethan read the headline with a smirk. He knew whose name was at the bottom of the article, he needn't look to see. He folded the paper in half, placing his letter to Cassandra into the outgoing slot.

"That was beautiful," he congratulated his brother, to himself.

"Bravo."

Ethan went back to his hotel room, preparing for checkout. He put the paper into his briefcase, then headed down to the lobby and left.

Stacy's eyes were sealed shut, at first. Slowly, they began to adjust, then allowed themselves to open. She felt different. Whatever had caused her grief before was incomprehensible. She appeared to be in some type of building, engulfed by shadows. There was a brightness coming from an open doorway in the front of the structure.

"Where am I?"

She asked herself aloud, stumbling towards the light.

Randy and his mom, also awoke in the dark.

"Mom?"

"I'm here, Randall. Follow my voice."

"What is this place?"

"I'm not sure, honey. Take my hand."

Like Stacy, what had led them to this new place was forgotten. They too headed into the radiating luster in front of them.

Chapter 2:
The Inception Of Rivalry

"I'm afraid we lost one," the doctor delivering the twins fretted to announce.

The mother of the brothers wept uncontrollably.

"May I...have t-the other?"

"There's, more..."

The sobs ceased, as the mother looked at the doctor with fear.

"The other one, well, he was born, apart. We have to piece him together."

Tears poured once more. The nurse attempted to ease the burden with a hug.

"We are doing all that we can for both," the doctor assured.

"Someone get me a chart of anatomy. I want to put this little guy together properly," one of the doctors ordered, while a second doctor went to work to try to revive the stillborn.

A nurse returned to the surgical room with the chart. The doctor cut a *Y* shaped incision into the infant, opening up his abdomen.

"Once we get all the organs in place, we will attach the limbs. First things first," the doctor uttered with concern, placing the internal parts beside where they needed to go.

Sixteen hours later, both twin brothers were brought in to their sleeping mother. A nurse gently awoke her.

"They're both healthy and alive. We are keeping them for observation, but I thought I would pass on the good news."

"Bless you," the mom of the boys repeatedly remarked, happy tears dripping down her cheeks.

A week after the miraculous was performed, the hospital released the newborns to the care of their mother.

"They both are precious. Spoil them every chance you get. They fought hard to be here. They're special, in all ways imaginable," the doctor declared upon the release of the patients.

The gratitude full mother kissed the docs and nurses on their necks, thanking them again, several times over.

The boys learned to walk, and talk, at the same moments. The first word for both of them being, "boom." Ian, from watching a character with a gun who hunted rabbits. Ethan, from the coyote who was always trying to make a speedy cuckoo explode.

Ian took a liking to chewing gum, writing short stories and long bike rides. Ethan, to creating flipbooks, a bit of pyromania and writing love poems to his crush, Cassie.

Cassandra was the girl next door. Ian liked her too, but he was a lot more interested in her step sister, Chloe. As their infatuations grew, so did their competition. Who could woo their girl with the sweeter text became a heavy part of their lives.

Chloe was treated unfairly by her step mom, often times taking the aggressive punishment on behalf of her sister. The girls shared a dad, but if he noticed the favoritism, he never lifted a finger to make it quit.

One morning, Ian found Cassandra sobbing in her backyard.

"Hey Cass, what's wrong?"

"It's Chloe."

Ian's heart sank. He knew whatever was coming next was not going to be pleasant.

"What about her?"

"She's dead."

Ian just stood there with his jaw open, unable to think. He was expecting the worst, or so he thought, but this was further than he expected the news to be. He took his latest short from his pocket, clutching it against his broken heart.

Autopsy results showed that Chloe had overdosed on fentanyl. Ruled as an accident, it was determined that she had mixed up her step mom's prescription with a bowl of sugar. Neither the twin boys nor Cassie, believed the death was accidental. She was murdered. It couldn't be proven, so it was never investigated.

Chloe's funeral was one of the only times that the brothers set aside their pettiness, both holding a hand of the grieving Cassandra.

Ian read his final story, before they lowered her six feet. He read it loudly, trying to keep his voice from cracking, wanting her last adventure to be heard clearly.

"Chloe, the brown haired, fair beauty, stepped off of her violet stallion. Her hair, flowed like soft strands of Heavenly vines in the breeze. The cool air kissed her cheek, she thought of her prince and smiled. She admired the scene that overlooked the cliff, she was young and in love, a maiden of perfection. Mere mirrors, could not reflect the amount of elegance she was given upon her creation. She was gracefully molded with care.

Today... ahem, sorry...

Today, was her wedding day. The gushing waterfall was gorgeous, but it could not compare to her. She mounted her stallion, heading to the palace where her prince was waiting. Crossing the Vortulmian Falls and braving the dangers there.

However, there was another. A foreboding villain, who wanted to crush the maiden's dreams. A foul creature, who caused many scars to adorn Chloe's angelic body."

He shot a hateful glance towards the one responsible for her not being here. The woman faking sorrow in the front row.

"When the palace came into the view of the young girl's ravishing blue eyes, the beast who delighted in the misery of the bride to be, stepped out from behind a tree trunk. Mad with love, Chloe withdrew her sword and removed the skull of her foe. It was the day she had dreamt of her entire life, nothing was stopping her from vowing to her lover, Ian. She rode up to the palace, the sun caressing her splendid, flawless smile, that shone like the winter snow. She was home... ahem... sorry.

She was home now, and there was no going back."

Claps arose, as did fretful sounds. The story was enchanting, but sadly it was never to be. His emotions broken in half, Ian folded the paper back up, returning to the side of his girl's sister. She hugged him with deep care, thanking him for the kind words about Chloe. Ethan joined the embrace, not out of jealousy but understanding.

Ian visited Chloe's grave almost daily. He glued the promise ring, that accompanied his concluding story, to her headstone. Nobody knew of the circle of commitment but him.

"I'll never meet another like you," he swore in the cemetery.

The day he presented the band to her resting place, was the same day that he met his destiny. While wiping his face dry, he was approached by a familiar stranger.

The approacher, was a man with seven knives protruding from his head and neck, as if a headpiece of blades. They weren't positioned horizontally around like a crown, but vertically as if a sideways orbit. Two on each side of his throat, two on either side of his ears and temples, and one sticking straight down through the top, penetrating his scalp. He wasn't wearing a top, showing that his chest was riddled with bullet holes.

Ian recognized the man from pictures his mother had around the house.

"You're my father, aren't you?"

The frightful visitor smiled at Ian, his features matching that of his and Ethan's.

"Pleasure to meet you, son."

"How?"

"I couldn't move on, without meeting my boys. I was trapped, within something called the Frahmasphere. I caught a glimpse of you both, when you were born. Caught between the Gray World and Second Chance, I was unable to greet you two. That is to say, somewhere between despair and hope, I was suspended. I tried to kill myself by stabbing these into my head, but it was too late. The bullet wounds took me at the precise time that the slits did. Since I neither died from suicide nor homicide, I was stuck in the void. The green mist that makes up the Frahmasphere. Not ready to cross over, but unable to qualify for Second Chance. I had to use your girlfriend's untimely demise as a portal back. Until I return, she lingers in my place. I will make my journey here quick, but first you must fetch Ethan. I have to show you each the paths for which you were conceived. With haste, you must learn the skills I will show."

"I have no words."

"It will all make sense, in time. I shall explain in better detail once you both are before me. Bring Ethan, but mention me not to your mother. Time is too short to waste. Your precious Chloe will wonder endlessly in the journey to the next. She is scared and confused. Save your damsel."

The following day, once the morning cartoons rolled their credits, Ian bribed his twin sibling to come with him to the cemetery.

"Ethan, my boy," the knife decorated man greeted.

"This can't be truthful. What kind of trick is upon me?"

"None, son. It is I. I have a present for you both."

Their father presented a bag. Inside, was a BB gun and a written memo on how to make bombs.

"Ian, you will practice your shooting, while I work with Ethan. When we are finished, I will teach you the art of stealth."

Two days were spent with each boy. They gained their knowledge quickly, taking to their specific set of expertise naturally.

On the fifth day, their dad placed his palms over this eyes, calling forth memories that he had long forgotten. Memories of the place that he referred to as Second Chance.

Second Chance, was one of many alternatives to the passing of life. He explained, that there was *The Event* and Heaven, Hell, Gray World and Second Chance. The latter, was where those who died prematurely went. Freak accidents, the murdered, all those aborted, born dead or taken out by their own hands went there. Those who went by natural causes or medical conditions, went to one of the other places. The only stipulation, was that only those under the age of 40 were permitted to phase two. Those over the hill, usually went to the other destinations with the peaceful passers and the sick.

"I was born alive though," Ian protested.

"Yes, but your condition is reminiscent of Second Chance. Remember your journey there to be enlightened. I hate to say, but my time is up, I must be going."

Each of his sons hugged him, then he pulled the knife from the top of his cranium out and slit his throat. An open door on fire appeared behind him, then he was taken into the darkness. Giving up himself, so that Chloe could escape the green vapor that ensnared her spirit.

"Remember your glimpses," he reminded them as the door slammed shut.

"So, we are the keepers of Second Chance?"

Ethan wondered aloud, to which Ian replied without clarity.

"We exist, to rival one another."

"When are we supposed to start the count?"

"We are ready now."

The two walked home not saying much. Ian hid away his gun, Ethan the instructions for building devices. They each had an agenda handed down by their father. He had given them a map, aside from his fatherly instructing.

"A secluded spot where you two can sharpen what I taught you," he made clear, a mere second before he was taken to Hell.

Later that night, Ian made due on his bribe. Switching rooms, Ethan peeked upon his girlfriend in a state of undress as she readied herself for bed. Something Ian had stumbled on by accident, quickly turning away in his faithfulness to Chloe. Ethan gazed with wonder, a wide grin across his prepubescent profile.

Chapter 3:
Second Chance And Dreamt Glimpses

Stacy walked down the ramp, entering her new reality. She looked back at the building she had just came out of, which had an aurora of digitalization just like the wooden slope that led down to the thumping path below. The path was layered with the beating of hearts that were buried just beneath the surface. They each pulsated in different rhythms, corresponding with what their former owners were enduring here. The red road scattered in various directions.

Lining the beating paths, was blue grass that scattered as far as the eye could see. Randomly placed within the grass, were hands that outstretched towards the green, sky above, that is the vaporish portal known as the Frahmasphere.

This world was without trees, at least in the sense of ones made from bark. Here, the forest was created by the lower limbs of those who dwelled in Second Chance. The legs were different in size, connected by the four base tissues within the human anatomy.

From the direction of the structure she had exited, she heard two gasps. She turned to her left to peer from her peripheral and caught the sight of two others emerging.

Ethan had hoped his spying would continue to unravel more of Cassie, once she turned off her light and they both closed their eyes to sleep for the night. Unfortunately for him, he was not given his want but his need.

When Ethan closed his eyes in the Earth realm, he opened them in Second Chance. The sound of rushing waters filled his eardrums.

"So much for the view," he muttered to himself, looking into the black around him.

This all seemed vaguely familiar to him, then he thought about his dad's words. It dawned on him where he was. He turned around, seeing a light emitting from the outside of where he was. He walked towards the colorful spectrum, stepping out.

He stepped to the edge of the incline, that extended away from where he had awoken. The waters, were five waterfalls that flowed into the same spot. The water wasn't clear nor blue but sparkling pink. The sky overhead was green. There were rocks lining the flowing streams, they varied in orange hues. It was a spectacular sight, but not the one he was desiring. No imagery of Cassandra.

His memory was triggered, he had been here before, before he first laid his eyes on his mother. He looked back to the shadows, nearly jumping when a voice called out to him.

"Ethan, come back into the safe house. It is dangerous out there."

Suddenly, Ethan found himself unable to speak. His inability wasn't temporal, it was taken away!

"Step inside. You won't be able to talk, but you can listen, which is more important now anyways."

Ethan walked back up the ramp. The other voice was soothing. He recalled it from the banks of his recollection. Standing in the doorway was a boy about the same age as Ian and him were back on Earth.

"You're in a flashback. Had you not stepped outside, you could still talk. I had a hard time figuring out which house we had met in, there's so many. I'm Ojeda. Guide of Second Chance. I was here when you died, you may not remember, but it's true."

Ethan listened to the Guide explain, his mind travelling nowhere. He couldn't remember the name of his crush, but he still knew his brother was Ian.

"Don't worry, you're not dead. When the hospital revived you, you were given a second chance on Earth. This realm, is different than the one you were given. Here, those who die before they were meant to are given the opportunity to grow old. However, there are dangers that dwell here. I call them Visculoquists. You are here temporarily, so you will not encounter them. Your brother and you have a special link to the ones the Visculoquists hunt. You can help them survive, if you choose to. Ian and yourself are the few that have visited here and went back. That is why you can communicate with the ones here."

Ian slept while Ethan did, he could hear the voice of Ojeda, but was trapped in his mother's womb. His subconscious took in what the Guide was saying. Déjà vu, sank into his thoughts. He had heard this all before, when he was at the youngest point of his life. This dream, was a refresher course for him.

"Most who come here never return to Earth. Their spirits, have the ability to grow as old as 40 years of Earthly age. Half a life span is better than a quarter of one, wouldn't you say?"

Ojeda giggled, finding the question humorous.

"Sorry, I kind of just had to. I rarely get to crack a joke, so I took advantage, my bad. Anyways, if you ever want to tap in, just squeeze your temples once, then tap them twice. Doing this, will enable the link. I got to go, as do you. Others have arrived."

Stacy turned her body full around, facing Randy and his mom.

"Are you new here too?"

The mom was too mesmerized by the extravagance of the scenery to reply. Randy took it upon himself to do it.

"We are. Where are we?"

"I'm not sure. I just... woke up here."

The nearest ensemble of legs began to move, making a sound like a thousand stomping feet.

"Quick, back into the safe house," a voice called out.

Stacy turned to run, but one of the hearts below her feet knocked her balance away. The same happened to Randy's mom. Stacy scrambled to her feet, helping up the other female.

Several of the forearms moved towards Randy's mother, holding her ankles to keep her from running up the ramp.

"What's going on?"

Randy inquired of the other boy, who was hidden away in the blackness.

"Stay inside. Ignore the screaming."

The connected limbs split, opening up. Stacy yelped, covering her mouth to keep more escaping shrieks from erupting.

"My mom, we have to help her!"

"It's too late!"

Randy attempted to run outside, but Stacy blocked him with her frame. He could hear his mom squealing for help, but he was helpless. After a few moments, the screeches stopped.

"Be glad you turned away," the third party assured.

"Who are you?"

"Ojeda the Guide of Second Chance. We have some things to go over. Have a seat, both of you."

Ian awoke, simultaneous with Ethan. The sun was rising in the east, chasing away the nightfall.

"Breakfast is ready," their mom informed from below.

They ate their biscuits and gravy, reflecting on the previous night's cache.

"Everything kosher with you two?"

"Just slept hard," Ian told her.

"Same here. Vivid dreams and all that," Ethan retorted.

"Well, you boys have a good day. I'm off to work."

She kissed their foreheads, picked up her keys, then began her day.

The twins rinsed their plates, placing them in the sink for later washing.

"Glad she is oblivious. What did you dream about?"

"Our births."

"So you also saw Second Chance?"

"Not saw, heard."

"Up for a day of practice?"

"No time like the present."

"Let the pre games begin."

"It's very rare to see adults, here. The Visculoquists have a harder time tracking innocence. The lower your age, the less of a threat they are. I'm sorry about your mom."

"A Visculoquist, is that what I saw come out of the many legs?"

"Indeed, Stacy."

"They're awful. Plain disgusting."

"I would wholly agree."

"What is this place?"

"As I stated before, Second Chance. In order for you two to be here, you would have had to expire."

"So, this is the afterlife?"

"One of them."

"How did we pass on? How come I cannot commemorate anything previous to this?"

"I'm simply a Guide. I don't have all the answers. But I will make fair warning, the Visculoquists can remember everything you don't. They will use your thoughts from before against you. Don't trust your eyes, even if they come in a form that you can think of and place as fact, they are the masters of trickery. Illusion is their game, banishment is their aim."

Chapter 4:

The Bunker, Flames Ablaze, Retaliation Equals Number One

No trespassing signs were staked all over the field where the map led the brothers.

"You sure this is a good idea?"

"Do you want to miss out on destiny?"

"No, but I worry that someone might see where we're headed and follow."

"Look around Ethan, there's not an eye for miles."

"Must be my nerves."

"Dad predicted as such, remember?"

"Yeah. Still a little wound from last night, I guess."

"Understandable. Do you think you'll feel guilty, ya know, the first time?"

"Not after our dream. Most of our victims get to keep living on. What about you, thinking about backing out now?"

"Letting you get all the glory? Fat chance, man."

Ethan laughed, Ian did too. They may have been on the road to trying to outdo one another, but they were brothers. Twins especially have an unbreakable bond. They loved each other, even if things were about to get darker, the light of love would still shine on.

"This is the spot," Ian pointed out.

Ethan removed the row of pebbles, revealing a handle. He pushed and pulled, until the ground gave way to a small opening below the stalks of corn.

"You ready?"

"Born so."

They slipped into the slot, replacing the faux entrance before descending. Once the entrance was slid shut, the lights to the bunker came on.

"Whoa," they both said, at the exact same time.

Half of the bunker was a shooting range, as well as places to practice stealth and escape scenarios. It was built with every possible outcome in mind. The other half, was a series of tables with equipment to make every bomb imaginable, complete with testing areas that burrowed into the ground so not to disturb the ground level.

"How many stories down do you figure it goes?"

"Enough to make us experts."

They split up to their respective sides, utilizing every inch of the educational playgrounds.

Explosives were detonated, as Ian conquered his learning curve, gaining smarts on how to shoot in any position without missing.

While holes were put dead in the center of each target, Ethan developed many ways to create bombs. If it could be used, it was accessible to the bomber in the making. The combinations seemed endless.

About a hour before their mom usually got off work, the brothers emerged from the bunker. They hid away the handle then headed home. Each with a deeper passion for their vices.

During the last week of school, Ethan and Ian were itching to try out their newfound knowledge.

"What have you learned?"

"How to defeat you."

"Shall see about that one!"

The boys spent their Summer break from school in the bunker. They furiously self taught themselves, read suggestions left to them by their father and matured in their pursuits.

One day, while making out with Cassie, Ethan pulled a lighter from his pocket.

"Feel like being bad?"

Cassandra howled like wolf, a dash of excitement in her eager eyes.

Ethan led her behind their middle school. Pulling a wad of paper from his pocket, he lit it on fire, then tossed it into what they both thought was a garbage bin. Within seconds, enormous flames arose from the receptacle.

"Wow! What's in there, bags of dried leaves?"

Ethan threw open the hatch, revealing an oil drum!

"I didn't expect that to be what this was," Ethan chuckled.

His arm around his girl, they watched the fire, aroused by the destruction. Ethan grabbed Cassie by her hips, then pressed his tongue into her mouth. The two made out, until the sounds of a fire engine filled their ears.

"We better go," Cassandra chortled.

Ethan's insides raged hotter than the burning barrel. The euphoria was exhilarating. Being with Cassie and exploring his hands was fun, but this, this was something else entirely! This, was significant to what he was told was his purpose. A taste of his destiny.

School returned in session in the Fall. By time they returned, they were masters in their crafts. They had only just begun, but they had found their calling. Woe to the world, to the other students, teachers and faculty. Something within the twins was unleashed, a fervor for bloodshed and a yearning to carry out their father's vision.

The first test of the school year, earned Ian his very first F-score. The teacher who gave him the low grade was Mr. Nusam, husband of the most hated teacher in school, Mrs. Nusam, who taught English.

One night, while the couple was away, Ian broke into the couple's home. Finding their rifle, he practiced shooting it without bullets to get a feel for the recoil. When they returned, he waited in their closet. As they ate dinner, he plotted his moves carefully. When the couple was finishing dessert, Ian shot Mr. Nusam in the head. When Mrs. Nusam got up to run, he placed the barrel of the duo's rifle under her chin, sprinkling her brain against the ceiling. It excited him with eroticism to watch their minds trickle downwards. Their murders were crucial in him finding the rifle as his weapon of choice.

The pair was witnessed in an intense squabble during their outing, causing the scene to be ruled as a murder-suicide. Not even Ethan figured Ian responsible, not until years later when he confessed it to him.

After hitting all the targets in a rapid succession, in the bunker the following day, Ian was rewarded with a secret compartment unfastening. Inside, he found a custom built sniper rifle. He vowed to carry out his dad's will using only it and nothing else.

The events solidified Ian and Ethan in their deadly habits. They had a taste of their life's works and it overtook them both. They spent most of their waking hours in the bunker, even sneaking out at night, taking turns covering for one another. They were obsessed with their studies. Nothing else mattered, even Cassandra became forgotten to an extent.

The twins drifted further apart, the older they got. Rarely speaking, captivated by their compulsions. Ian's infatuation with being a skilled marksman, and Ethan's fetish with becoming a demolition expert, caused the two to attend different high schools. They wouldn't have any communication with one another, until the day of their graduations. When that time came, their challenge against each other took a serious turn.

Chapter 5:
Stacy's Deceit

Randy held Stacy's hand, fearful of what he would see leftover from his mother. They walked down the ramp. Not stopping, but inspecting the pillar that was once his mom at the base as they hurried past it.

"Careful where you step, Randall. The path can cause you to lose your footing."

The young boy listened to Stacy's warning, treading lightly as to not step on the thumping hearts. He stopped and looked back at the pillar. His mom's face in mid scream, she was turned towards the safe house, one hand reaching for it.

"What happened to her?"

"I'm not sure. We have to stay vigilant, so it doesn't happen to us."

Randy nodded, looking at the teenage girl like his new mom. He was in her care now, of that, he was sure.

They walked along the beating path, shifting their eyes from side to side to ensure the forearms weren't in motion. They were stationary, as were the intertwined legs. With the dangers aside, Second Chance was stunning.

The two walked for miles, passing thousands of upper and lower limbs. Eventually, they came upon a small strip of buildings that looked digital with the way their outlines stood out from their colors. One was a bookstore, one was a toy store and one was a gym. None of them were grand in size, similar to the safe houses.

"Can you read, Randall?"

"Not yet."

"Interested in learning?"

Randy, whose eyes were fixated on the toys, shook his head to deny the offer. Stacy stifled a laugh.

"Want to have a look at the toys?"

"Yes, please! Oh, please, yes!"

The wood to the toy store was yellow in tint. They walked up the two steps, entering the shop.

There were a few other kids about Randy's age inside. They ignored the newcomers, until Stacy engaged with them.

"Hello, I'm Stacy. This is my friend, Randall."

The kids smiled at them both, then turned back to their toys.

"Is there an owner of this place?"

Her question went unheard.

"Randall, why don't you look around while I try to find a shopkeeper."

Randy didn't need to be told twice, turning to the displays of toys with animation. His retinas overwhelmed, fingertips tingling.

Stacy walked around the counter to the backroom.

"Oh hey," Ojeda greeted.

"You're the Guide and the shopkeeper?"

"There's no keeper. The fabrication known as currency is not a thing in this realm."

"What are you doing here?"

"Just checking up on you newbies. I figured you'd eventually find your way here."

"I see. You're not allotted past the bounds of the buildings, are you?"

Stacy asked the question as it occurred to her.

"Correct. I can teleport between them, even go out to the ends of the ramps and steps, but that's all."

"Well, it was a pleasure running in to you again. I think a toy is just what Randall requires to get his mind off his mom."

"Have at it. I suggest only one, two may gain unwanted attention."

"Understood," Stacy affirmed, shivering at the image of the Visculoquist she had seen.

Ojeda seemed distracted. Stacy walked out from the backroom.

"Randall?"

Stacy panicked, seeing the store barren. She rushed outside, finding him playing with a stuffed animal. The other kids were nowhere within range of their sight.

"Randall, you had me worried," Stacy scolded, reminding Randy of his mother.

"My apologies."

"You picked a toy, let's keep moving."

"Ugh. Only one?"

"Yes. Are you sure that is the one you want?"

"Let me double check," Randy responded, running back inside.

"Kids," Stacy snickered to herself.

"Babe?"

The voice of a man inquired, causing a part of Stacy's hall of thoughts to light up. A memory arose in her head as she spun around.

"Oh my God."

"It is you!"

Stacy stood dumbfounded, remembering the face of the guy who had just stepped out from the gym. His muscles glimmered with sweat, making Stacy bite her lower lip. She was shocked to see the one who was her first love, not recalling his abandonment of her for Hannah.

"Baby, I've missed you so badly. I couldn't live without you by my side, so I came to find you."

"I never thought I'd ever see you again."

"Well, here I am, babe."

"I just... I don't know what to say."

"Then keep silent and walk with me."

Her ex put out his hand, which she took without hesitation. Forgetting about Randy, she left the strip of buildings.

They chatted while strolling, stepping on pounding hearts and not noticing. Stacy's mind could think of nothing but the glistening muscles of her first. She missed his smile, feeling so lucky to be able to regard his handsomeness again.

He led her to the five flowing waterfalls, staying far away from the safe house where Ethan had met Ojeda.

"It is beyond Utopia to stare into your eyes, baby," he wooed her.

"I feel the same. I've always been crazy about you."

"True. You were head over heels from day one."

Stacy bashfully turned away.

"Don't look away, babe. Keep those eyes on me."

"Stacy?"

Randall called out over and over, looking for his mentor. When he realized she had left him, he sat down and bawled, clutching his cow plush.

The plush was black and white with striped legs, some checkered patterns, a red scarf and some polka dot patterns.

"Put your arms around me, baby. I need your touch."

Stacy did so immediately, hugging her ex tightly. Suddenly, the man began to jerk violently, his flesh giving way to brain cells. His arms and legs seemingly melted, leaving only veins which entangled the horrified Stacy. Out from the mind neurons, protruded his organs that now were placed on the outside of his torso. His head snapped back, then vanished. His vocal organs sat on the outside of his throat, moving when he spoke.

"Hold me, darling."

Stacy strained her own speech organs, realizing she had been duped by a Visculoquist. The veins holding her in place began to bleed onto her, turning her spirit to stone. When she was nothing more than a pillar, just like Randy's mom, the Visculoquist let go.

Chapter 6:
Connecting With Chloe, Graduation Day Escalation

Seven days prior to his graduation, Ian pressed his temples then tapped them twice, returning to Second Chance.

Ethan was too preoccupied to carry on his relationship with Cassie, who had become a victim of her own addiction to astronomy. The two parted ways on the same day that Ian sought out Chloe, unbeknownst to them all.

Ian opened his eyes, taking in the noise from a babbling brook. He made his way into the brightness of the realm, unsure what to expect. Cast upon a background of orange hued cliffs, the effervescent waters flowed into one of the waterfalls that Ethan saw when he had last visited a decade prior. Within the waters swam human entrails. They slithered like water moccasins, using their long, tube bodies.

"How crude," Ian mumbled to himself.

He turned from the waters, catching sight of Chloe, who had grown up, just like him. She was running from a swarm of forearms, that were chasing her like disturbed hornets. He tried to call out to her, but was denied because a few of the swimming intestines had coiled around his neck. Trying to pry the slimy vines away was useless. They pulled him into the waters. He rode the current to where the waterfalls met.

Fighting to catch a breath, he was dunked to the floor of the stream bed. He took in the sights of hundreds of pillars, among them was

Randy's mom and Stacy. When he passed out from drowning, he awoke back in the Earth realm.

Ethan put on his cap and gown, then headed to the place where his graduation was being held. When he arrived, he shook hands with his friends, thankful his mom wasn't attending but wishing she could be.

The twins' mother had died a year earlier from complications with cancer. Her fight had been long and tough. She passed away, alone. The brothers were busy in the bunker when she pleaded for them to assist her. She was found slumped over beside her bed, signs of her struggle very apparent.

"You ready for your big day?"

Ethan's favorite teacher asked him.

"More than you know," he replied to her with a double meaning.

"I'm sure your mom would be proud."

"She is. Dad will be too."

The teacher gave him an embrace. While he took his seat, the ceremony began. Several speeches were given, Ethan listened to each intently.

"Here's to the rest of our lives," the valedictorian smiled, finishing her address.

One by one, names were called and diplomas were handed out. When they were completed, the graduates moved their tassels from right to left. They all stood up, except for Ethan, to throw their caps into the air.

As Ethan fled the ceremony, a dozen explosions blasted behind him. He had placed enough to wipe out everyone in attendance. Being the sole survivor was a must. He ran to a vehicle he had on standby, one unregistered, leaving his own at the scene.

He drove away, the ground still shaking from the ongoing detonations. He drove by a row of ambulances and Police cars, pulling over to the side to allow their passage. The car in front of him had also pulled to the side, which helped him to blend. Once the vehicles with the sirens were parked, he waited until the second round started to erupt before continuing away. He imagined his dad smiling up at him and felt proud.

After two straight hours, the bombs stopped. A bulldozer was used to pile the charred beyond recognition, then they were cremated on site.

A memorial was held for the students, teachers, parents and other relatives, friends and other attendees who were tragically taken out that day. None were suspected to have survived the attack. Baffled, the investigation returned no results. The case stayed open for a decade after.

Across the city, Ian straightened his cap. Looking at his reflection in the mirror, he ran his palms down the creases of his gown in an attempt to flatten them out. He drove his car to where his graduation was held.

His connection to his brother told him what had occurred. He knew emergency response would be tied up there, which bought him plenty of time to carry out his own acts of violence.

Speeches were read, a valedictory text was read aloud by the top of their class and tassels were moved from one side to the other. Being the last to go, Ian slipped into a tunnel he had pre-dug for his escape, after he received his diploma.

Several shots rang out, then many more. From the two towers surrounding the ceremony, a rifle customized to sense movement shot attendees, while Ian manned the one his dad had built. Bullets tore through caps and gowns, wounding a ton, killing even more. The unmanned rifle was also set for head shots apart from only sensing movements, an invention left to him from his father.

Those who survived the first rifle, were gunned down by Ian. He left a few stragglers alive so that he wouldn't be a suspect when found. Unlike Ethan, being a known survivor was necessary for him.

He buried his sniper rifle in his trunk, then returned to where his seat was. Perfectly timed, as two bullets hit him in the shoulder from the gun in the first tower. Once the timer was up, the evidence in tower one dissipated, another invention left by dad.

Being seen as a victim, Ian's car was never searched. He returned for it, once he was discharged from the ER. Cops questioned him during his stay, but like the others, he claimed to not be able to recall much before being shot.

He drove his vehicle away from the place of his mass murder, the blood droplets still fresh. He was grinning. He pictured his dad applauding what he had done, imagining him praising the genius method in which he planned it all. Ian had covered his tracks well with the hole he snuck to tower two through, which investigators deemed to be made from animals, not the person, or persons, responsible.

Funerals were held for those who were loss on the day of celebration from student to adulthood. Ian attended from a distance, rifle to his shoulder. The massacre wasn't over yet. Firing then moving, moving then firing, the panicking goers couldn't pinpoint from where the shots were coming from. They dropped like clay targets, scattered across the cemetery like leaves during the Fall season.

An extensive investigation was performed, with hours wasted. Who was responsible went undetected. It was believed to be the work of a group of gunmen, not the work of a solo shooter. To this very day, the case was never closed, nor were any further details ever uncovered.

Ian and Ethan moved far away from where they carried out the beginning of their terrorist acts. Ian began his career as a reporter for the Circadian. Ethan, presumed to be deceased, lived off of the death benefits of their mother's insurance. The checks were deposited in Ian's name, but Ethan easily cashed them. It wasn't an act of kindness from Ian, but a requisite for their work to carry on. Ethan getting busted for his graduation exterminations, meant Ian could not compete with him for higher numbers. The competition needed to be fair, for the proper glory and gloating to occur.

Seven days post graduation, Ian returned yet again to Second Chance. He searched high and low for Chloe, but her whereabouts couldn't be identified. There were too many spirits this time thanks to the work of him and his brother. The paths of hearts were lined with the same pillars he had seen previously below the falls.

He grabbed a running young teen, trying to figure things out.

"What's your name?"

"Randy."

"I like that cow, he have a name?"

"Spot."

"Good choice, fitting," he determined, noticing the polka dots inside the plush's ears.

"What happened here?"

"The Visculoquists!"

Figuring an explanation too long, Ian didn't ask what the teen meant.

"Do you know somebody named Chloe? She would be about my age."

"Chloe, yeah. That's the name of the lady who found me after I was abandoned by Stacy."

"Can you lead me to her?"

"I don't know where she is now. I haven't seen her for a long minute. I gotta get to the safe house. I suggest you come with me, lest you are turned to a pillar."

"Listen Randy, can you do me a favor?"

"I guess," Randy sighed, undoubtedly rolling his eyes, though the expression couldn't be seen in the gloom of the building he had ran into.

"Find Chloe. Tell her, Ian is trying to reach her."

"Fine."

"Take care, Randy. I hope we can one day we meet again. I'll be back."

"When? You know, in case Chloe should ask?"

"Two weeks from today. Do you have a way to keep track?"

"No time, here."

"I'll find you, you find Chloe."

"Sounds like a pact."

Ian pressed, then tapped twice, reawakening from his out of body experience. He put in a stick of nicotine gum then mounted his bicycle. He had started smoking after finding a pack in the bunker. Once he saw the toll it took on his mother, he decided to try to quit. Being a lifelong chewer thus far, he relied on the gum to dull his cravings. All it did was replace one addiction with another. At least the new one was less likely to lead to the miserable way in which he and Ethan found their mom.

Chapter 7:
The Game, Part One

Now that the brothers had their taste of mass slaughter, the game had began. A vicious contest was underway just as their dad foretold.

Ethan returned to the bunker once, blowing it to smithereens. Any trace of their past, he wanted to erase. Ian approved. The only direction to go was forward. Onwards to new frontiers, progressing their shared intimacy for thrill killing.

On a random date in July, kids were creating castles of sand, girls were working on tans while guys were playing frisbee on the beach and fishing off the docks. Laughter could be heard up and down the shoreline, when suddenly one of the frisbee throwers combusted into a display of blood and fire. Then another. The onlookers began to frantically scramble, as more landmines were activated. Splattered with red, the sand was washed away by the tide, turning the ocean the same shade briefly.

Shark fins could be seen near the shore soon after. A man, with the last name of Nil, fell overboard his fishing vessel during the attack, causing his head to be eaten by a large Great White.

Good samaritans tried to help evacuate the bloody seashore, only to be blown to bits. Those who did survive were left without limbs. Some, died soon after.

Ian wrote about the attack on the coastline, earning him the badge of star reporter. The event went viral, making national news. Disabling the location tracker on his work phone proved useful. He made his typical claim to be in the right place, right time. In actuality, he was hundreds of miles away, about to unfold his own incident. He had dreamt the bloody shoreline and filled in the details based off his brotherly intuition.

Two sodas were laid on the gas station counter.

"Will that be all for you?"

"No, let me also get twenty on...," the customer turned to see what pump he had parked at, when blood and brains from the clerk sprayed his face.

He tried to make it to his vehicle, but was also shot. A pregnant woman floored her car to try to get away when she too took a bullet in the noggin. Luckily, the baby survived the ordeal and was rescued by first responders.

Thirty minutes later, a different gas station was shot up by Ian, leaving five dead and two in critical condition.

Another half hour after the second attack, a third happened. This time, there were no survivors. Among the dead were the reacting paramedics, who Ian stuck around to execute before leaving his post.

"So it begins," Ethan declared to his TV turning from the news to cartoons.

"Mweep-mweep," a speedy bird was calling out from the speakers.

Ethan decided to pen a letter to Cassandra.

'Lovely Cassie,

What a world we live in, eh? Seems like the planet on which we live grows more violent by the day. It is a wonder anyone can keep sane.

Congratulations on your acceptance into the Space Program! At last, your dreams are becoming reality. I am so very proud of you! I hope that means something...

I received your condolence postcard regarding mother, which touched me deeper than you can guess. She was a wonderful person. It is a shame that her practices sealed her demise.

Ian says hello. We are both doing well and living out our own destinies. He is always trying to upper hand me, you know how he is. Haha. I would have loved to see him and Chloe get hitched, maybe have their own set of babies. Pathetic is the hand dealt by life more often times than not.

With affection,

Ethan.'

He sealed the letter, putting a bogus return address in the left corner of the envelope. Cassandra was unaware that he was supposed to be lifeless, but he couldn't risk being intercepted. Thanks to father, him and Ian had long removed their fingerprints, so any attempt to trace it back would be pointless, minus his name. He never signed his last name, only the first. How to change his handwriting was even a craft passed down. If it was detrimental to evasion, the bunker taught it to the twins.

Ian cleaned his rifle, a hunk of nicotine gum in his cheeks. He sat back and watched the sun fade away with swirls of yellow and maroon. Many who thought they'd witness the same, were cut short of their thoughts by the fired bullets that day.

Once the sky turned black, he turned on his own television set.

"Shhh. Be vewy vewy quiet," the hunter was saying to the screen.

There's something in nostalgia that soothes the soul. The brothers were no different about it. The cartoons took them back to a simpler time, before worry about capture was even thinkable. Before they met their dad. Before mother was found seized up with her comforter in hand, her veins protruding from struggle.

Ethan was transported to Second Chance during a dream. He had initially thought himself within a safe house, but when he tried to find the light, there was none. He seemingly had no senses but touch, be could barely wriggle, confined. His surroundings rumbled. Eventually, he was permitted to move.

His arms and legs felt funny. He had no eyes to see, ears to hear or a tongue to speak. He could feel his heart beating, from somewhere else. He attempted to move his fingers but they were also gone. He felt confused, trapped within this new form. This unknown form!

He could feel his lungs breathing, then detach. Once his lungs were separated, he could see colors but not images. He could tell where the blue grass was, but not where the red heart paths were. He could see the outlines of the forearms and forelegs, because they reflected the green from the Frahmasphere.

He felt little flutters all over his new body. He had tried to get in to entomology to impress Cassandra once. Due to his knowledge in the field, he knew that his lungs were part moth! When the lungs saw moving green outlines of spirits, they became attracted to them. Still attached to his main frame via an umbilical cord, the lungs led him to wards the fleeing fugitives. He wasn't in control of himself, he was part of a greater presence, one combined with the parts of others. The main frame wasn't skin, but brain cells and stems. They almost seemed telepathic with the one he was hunting, his thoughts told him that the spirit he was chasing was... his mom!

When he caught her, he wrapped his stringy limbs around her, absorbing the life from her soul. He felt her harden as she stiffened to a pillar.

Ian was sharing the dream with his twin. He was pleading Ethan to stop, but he would not. Ian knew that he was now his mom. This was what she was going through after curling up on the floor in agony. He ran, but she was too slow. When the veins contorted around his frame, he felt all of his organs, which were in individual positions of one another, start to fail. His soul lost touch with the organs as they became stone.

He watched through her eyes, as Ethan sifted back to a tree of legs. He watched for hours, it felt like an additional lifetime. A burning sensation overcame him, then he started to dissipate. He wasn't breaking free of the horror, she was reforming on the bed of the pink waters. Though he was his mother, he was still aware that he was beneath the five waterfalls. The constant tingling stopped, giving way to a feeling of drowning. The waters suffocated him, yet he couldn't die. This wasn't Hell, but it might as well have been. It was certainly eternal suffering. Her suffering.

The brothers awoke simultaneously, both soaked in piss and sweat. Both, equally aware of what the other had dreamt.

Ian wished for a cigarette, a single hit, but he knew better. He felt a new sympathy for his mom, who experienced a dreadful end, only to continue in distress. He devoured through two rows of gum trying to find a fraction of ease.

Ethan felt the same anxiety, turning to what his dad always had, the drink. He gave a hundred bucks for a bottle since it was the after hours of the times for sales of alcohol. He was desperate to try to erase what he had just went through. The drink was salty, as he drank his tears along with each tip back. When he was hammered, he felt a small percentage of courage return. Still, he couldn't shut out the terror he and Ian had endured, both through the Visculoquist and their mother. Thanks to the infinite link of being fraternal siblings, the two divided their feelings. One of the vicarious happenings would have been frightening enough, but the pair of them equaled trauma. Even in their waking thoughts, they relived the dream from time to time.

One of the tally marks, among the handfuls of tallied victims, was named Norval Portiis. Norval was a time traveler from a parallel future, one segregated from Second Chance. Due to this outsider's untimely passing, Portiis was sent to an existence a few coordinate degrees away from the one of Stacy and Randy. His realm had a thinner veil, presenting new and unique dangers.

Norval woke up in a cave. He followed a sparrow of human veins and was led to a finger of one of The Aboriginables. It was heavy, far larger than Portiis, but because he was within the lateral version, he was basically a super soul. The finger was extremely sharp, so he used it as a blade. He sawed down the forearm trees, building a boat of sorts, linking the fore-leg flowers together for oars. When it was leak proof, he set sail against the red current, fighting entrails that acted as tentacles. After a couple of epic battles against the swimming guts, Norval made it to the mouth of an ocean. Only there were no waters nor life. In place of a horizon of waves was a massive worm farm. Instead of worms, there were miles and layers of intestinal tracts, wriggling like severed tongues.

The wife of the fisherman whose head became shark mush began to seek out the responsible. Sitting on the dock, she would pop her eyes from their sockets. While they dangled, her inner self escaped her body. Once free of her shell, she could see across the plains of the dimensions. Heaven and its splendor of gold and emeralds. Gray World and its despair, where those who still sought closure go. Hell, its caverns of fire and insects. The realm of *The Event*. She could see the lurkers and their various destroyers. There were entities in uncountable numbers. There were veils and splits that doubled the number of the entities. There were also reflecting realms and hemorrhaging ones. The stories that could be told from them all could wrap the Earth several times. The scenery was overwhelming so she clung to her task. It drove her forward.

She was now in spirit. Her name, Parzule, meant nothing to her in this form. Her mission was her purpose. She searched through the realms, along with the parallel worlds, trying to find the head of her husband. His wailing kept her up at night, it was distance and never ceasing.

She had to find his body first, which was buried by The Cloaks of Gray World, slowly turning to vapor. She would never find closure until both body and cranium were recovered. If they first turned to vapor then he would wander forever, alone. She would continue to seek, never to find.

She glided in the shadows, keeping from sight and the sights. She stumbled her way to a tree of flowing tears, the droplets that splashed against her lips still tasted of salt. She cried out to the weeping tree until it wept with blood. Out from the crimson falls, dropped the headless corpse belonging to her lover. Her spirit was led to the tree by the one that speaks with the wind, whose limbs end in anvils. She had to drag the body across the interdimensional lands, dodging their dangers. Each realm was tinted a different color, she knew that the Earth was without color for it bore all the shades in its realm.

The anvil handed thing then led her to a gateway back to Earth. She was then instructed to enter a black hole, awaking a dormant eternal being. She was sucked into the being, temporarily flowing along black waters. When she came out in Earth, she exited up through the ocean, swimming with the decapitated cadaver.

She carried her deceased husband to the dock where her physical form was. Her eyes were then replaced with care, as she left the trance known as Gormyzule. A practice that would pass down for the duration of Earth's existence.

Chapter 8:
The Game, Part Two

Ian participated in a marathon. Marking the last time that he would ever ride an actual bike. He came in second place by time it was finished. The entire ride, he was plagued with flashbacks of the nightmare that he and Ethan had. His eternally suffocating mother turned asphyxiated pillar would run backwards alongside him. The other competitors, turned from cycling pillars to external organ adorned beings without heads. He went through three whole packs of nicotine gum during the marathon's duration. He came in second because of his desire to get through the race of madness and away from the hallucinations. There are many layers to Hell, the rekindling of traumatic stress is surely one of them.

The passengers obeyed the light that told them to buckle up as the plane began to prepare for ascension. Some slept, others twisted the little dial that turned on the flow of air. Movies were turned on, books were opened. The plane began to accelerate, climbing in altitude. The seat belt light turned off, when it did the plane blasted into a ball of flames. Debris fell like rain, among it were burnt body segments.

Ethan admired the tragedy, a look of content across his expression. Another explosion occurred, followed by a few more. The tiny flows of air were worthless when the sky was full of fire. Plane pieces, body parts and other various forms of litter fell from the blasts, thumping against roofs. At least three homes had bodies impaled on their antenna roofs. Those with pools saw splashes. A few car wrecks also resulted from smashed windshields and swerves to miss sudden obstacles in the roadway.

Ethan clapped giddily.

"Second Chance, I am overflowing you," he cackled.

Ethan was his name, despair was his game.

Screams in amusement parks aren't uncommon, nor are loud noises at such places. Cotton candy was being eaten, stuffed animals being won and funnel cakes treated as delicacies. Ian watched it all unfold through the scope. He focused on the overpriced gift shop first, but decided it too simple.

A car of thrill seekers slowly drudged up a cloud high hill, klanking as a system of wheels and pulleys lifted it up. When it stopped at the top, the skulls of the front two tourists drenched the people behind them with red slush. The car toppled over the edge, barreling downwards, while more shots removed skull fragments.

A tower with seats sat suspended, waiting to drop its occupants. When it did, heads were blown off. The moderator thought nothing of the shrieks, until a flap of bloody skin slapped him in his face. He peeled the slab away, vomiting on his brand new shoes.

"Wascally wabbits," Ian imitated.

He put bullets in carousel commuters, gift shop perusers and theme park staff. The trigger was pulled without discrimination. Many flooded out the turnstiles, but he was already positioned to handle evacuation, murdering a handful of others as they tried to liberate themselves.

Both occurrences made national headlines. Speculations were given, slandering the innocent. States of emergency were declared. Schools let out early, along with some job sites. The country was in the palms of the twin brothers, trembling with panic.

"Could your next visit to the market conclude your life?"

One newscaster apprised, with the other sources quoting the same script.

"Authorities have no leads. The perp could be a parent, your neighbor, maybe even a personality in you that you're unaware of."

Doors were triple locked, sick time was put in, vacation days taken. The next assault could literally happen at any time, any place. Sheer trepidation may be another layer of Hell. Anyone who lived during phase two of the brother's game wouldn't dare to disagree.

"Nice work, same timer."

"Splendid masterpieces."

Each brother admired the doing of the other, despite their trivial contest.

Lovely ladies strutted onstage, all of them striving for the crown. Men whistled. Judges held up numbers that rated the contestants. Pulsating music played. The runway paved the way for lust. Those in attendance were drunk in varying ways.

When the show reached its close, the contenders lined up on the stage anticipating to see who would be crowned. Suddenly, rapid popping sounds filled the auditorium. The audience began to trample over themselves, trying to avoid being next. The stage was cluttered with beautiful women, who were leaking from their foreheads.

"Wabbit season," Ian parodied to himself.

With the doors chained shut, the frenzied mob were easy prey. No survivors lived through the calamity.

Ethan was at the mall, intending to purchase electronics that he could convert, when the sound of heavy artillery permeated. At first, he assumed it was Ian. Then, he saw the shooter who was not his other half.

"Egad," he caricatured.

Sneaking up behind the psycho with an uzi, he disarmed the assassin and bashed a VCR against his face until there was nada to recognize. The act wasn't done out of heroism but spite. He found strong offense in a third player entering the game.

Ian approved, writing an article about the hero whom had done what the law could not. His headline read:

'Brave Man Puts An End To Spree.'

The article referenced a series of violent crimes carried out by the gunner. It insinuated that the shooter could have been behind some of the twin's attacks. Lots of folks wanted a scapegoat and they had found him.

Though Ethan remained unnamed, he was hailed just the same. To celebrate, Ethan carried out the attack on the capitol. The bombing of congress rocked the nation. The terrorists were getting bolder was how the incident was perceived. Sources stated the attackers were retaliating for being publically outed. Nothing was off limits now in the minds of the public. Everybody was a target.

"Violent crimes continues to escalate, leaving many to wonder, who's next? The commander-in-chief? A class of kindergarteners? At what point, does our government step in to say, enough is enough?"

It was clear that the public opinion was reaching the media. Safety felt extinct. Any inclination that something was being done to end the insanity held no merit. Many took to the streets to protest, some tried their hand at copycatting.

The head of FBI held an emergency press conference for the matter.

"Everything that can be done is being carried out. We understand the circumstances are intimidating, but hope must remain. Believe in your government's effectiveness to handle these things. This is far from the first time that domestic terrorism has been endured. Like times past, it too will falter."

The agent's frontal lobe ruptured, causing him to fall dead at the podium. The press leaped from their chairs, flaring in to chaos. The cameras panned to the direction of the shots, but the perpetrator proved to be overly skilled. Using the effect of ricochet, Ian appeared to be legion. Sanguine fluid flowed in streams from the cadavers that piled around the FBI platform. The cameras cut away to standby screens, once their operators were slain.

Portiis abandoned his ship of limbs, setting forth on foot. Some of the field of intestines were serpents. Norval chopped them up with the sharpened finger, which only grew more of the squirmy guts.

Norval wasn't aware that he was dead, thinking that the dynamic of his travels had caused a malfunction. He placed himself in a dimension of Earth, so he still feared death.

After walking across acres of squishy bowels, Portiis watched the ground open up before him. Climbing out of the chasm, was a ten foot shard of jagged metal. The Aboriginable, to whom the weapon of Norval belonged. Tungnoch The Tiller, was the title of the alloy brute. Given the surname, because of his cultivation of butchered Miscreation bits.

Norval's nosed began to pour blood then formed a message from The Tiller.

'Drop the blade,' the blood formed.

"It is my only defense. Without it, I am prey to you."

His nose had clotted during his denial, but then Tungnoch wrote again using Norval's profusely dripping nostrils.

'With it, you declare war!'

Tungnoch's wrists begin to whirl, making his attached fingers rotating blades of serration. He slammed down towards Norval, hacking up the stomach worms.

Portiis' sinuses gushed, but he remained fixated on his opponent. He tripped, falling face first into the slimy viscera. His fall saved him from being a split spirit. Tungnoch lunged and got one of his arms stuck in the ground, which Norval used to his advancement. Swinging the weapon,

Norval attempted to disconnect the wrist using Tungnoch's digit. Being made of the same metallics, the damage was scarce.

'You lose,' a red rapid spelled out.

The ground behind Norval shifted, opening up an additional gully moisturized by slippery grubs. Out from the crevasse, a mastodon of green moss emerged. From its trunk, orange webs sprayed out in streams. When the slung entanglements wrapped around the arms of Tungnoch, they burrowed rips across the metal, spilling forth rust.

Tungnoch tried to return the attack, but was looped in innards. The defensive entrails slid along the shreds, then segmented off. The Aboriginable attempted to rid his wounds in vain.

Norval fled the confrontation, leaving the ancient rivalries to settle their differences.

Parzule snuck into the refrigeration unit of the store, the workers were gone for the weekend. She stripped off her clothing then entered the icy area. She sat down and flipped her eyelids inside-out. While she froze in place, her spirit manifested itself from the freezing skin suit, taking form as a giant soul stepping through the seas. This ritual, she called Szaijra.

She saw the sandy floor beneath the waters, underneath the otherworldly glass face of the waters, that was lined with buried spirits. They were the ones lost at sea, trapped in the waters, slowly turning to vapor. Anchors held each ensnared spirit to the depths. They had not passed on, they were just lost at sea. The spirits called out in a choir of whimpering, a hum of sobs, making it hard for her to find her husband. They wanted the help she was seeking to provide. They were pleading for closure.

Among the spirits were schools of Great Whites, each holding a human skull in their bellies. She used her claws to dig into the sharks. Not wanting to slaughter them, but having no choice. Her mate needed closure as did she, she would stop at nothing. Their love was without bounds.

Pirate souls fought tentacled creatures, while the soul of Parzule sought her hubby's cranium via ripped up shark contents. She had to dodge the thrusts of swords and the releases of ink poisonings as she skimmed. After an acre of maiming, she found the missing piece.

Fighting against avenging sharks, her spirit chewed up her foes as she sludged towards the shore. One claw swam forward, the other clenched her lifeless mate. When she reached the surface, her eyelids unflipped and she sat holding the headless corpse in the center of the freezer. Covered in salt, she began to thaw.

Chapter 9:
Perilous Times, Two Strangers

Ojeda looked upon the endless pillars in dismay. The Visculoquists were winning. He looked to the Frahmasphere then realized that it was getting closer to the ground level. If it reached it, worlds would collide. Intersections were usually twice as savage. This place was rough enough on its own. He felt something had to be done, but stood clueless.

By the Guide's side was Randy. By Randy, Spot. There was no judgment here. Nobody to make fun of a teen boy still finding comfort in a plush cow. Cruelty was a lost weapon, rightfully so, since most of the inhabitants were brought here because of it.

"They've never been this strong," Ojeda said with worry.

"What do you think it causing it?"

"Ethan and Ian."

"No way," a woman's voice butted in.

They were both startled by her sudden chime in. She stepped out from inside the safe house, joining the conversation holders at the top of the incline.

"Gosh, what a ghoulish entrance," Randy huffed, his heart pumping harshly in the path somewhere.

"Spirits turned to stone, Visculoquists gaining unfound strength and I'm what makes you jump?"

"Whatever," Ojeda mumbled.

"You're Chloe," Randy realized aloud.

"Have we met?"

Randy held up Spot, then she knew. The child had grown quick.

"Turns out the kid is pretty tough after all...

Been awhile," she stated with a quick rising of her eyebrows.

"He's been looking for you."

"You know Ian?"

"Yeah. Up until two years ago, he used to come once a week, Earth time."

"Really? Such a charmer."

"Where have you been, Chloe?"

"Hiding."

"Where?"

"Where the Visculoquists do."

"What a load," Ojeda interrupted, rejoining the talk.

"It's true. Do legs see? They only house one entity at a time. Any energy goes. When they're sealed, the others just pass by. The buildings aren't the only safe places."

"Genius," Randy re-entered.

"I've been looking for Ian too."

Now, neither of the males had anything to say.

"There's a teleport inside one of the forelegs."

"You're just now coming forward with such knowledge?"

"It isn't that simple. When I return, I am somebody else, like a puppeteer."

"Or a Ventriloquist…"

"Precisely."

"You never found him, after so many years of seeking?"

"No. All I found was Ethan's obituary."

"Oh?"

"He was killed during a mass bombing on his graduation day."

"No, he wasn't, " Ojeda tagged in.

"How can you be sure?"

"I'm the Guide. I meet everyone who comes here. I only met the twins on the day of their births. Then just Ethan, long after."

"If that's the reality, then?"

"Then, they're the cause of this. All of this," Oneda explained, placing his palms up towards the green vapor sky.

Six eyes met, nobody had anything else to add.

Ian knotted his tie, looking at himself in the mirror. Tonight, he would see the face of his other half. Driving his latest piece of junk, he sped to the bistro.

"I'd recognize a face like that anywhere," Ethan grinned, putting his arms out for a welcome squeeze.

"Corny as ever," Ian chuckled trying to return the tighter grasp.

Once they quit their foolish behavior, they went inside and were seated.

"Take a look over the menus. I'll be with you in a moment," the waitress announced, catching Ian's eye.

"Ahem. Haven't seen you look at a girl like that since Chloe."

"You haven't seen me around any girls since Chloe."

"Ahhh, but I do... know you."

"Perhaps, same timer. Perhaps."

"I assume, you have noticed the ante being raised?"

"Can I get you anything?"

The waitress inquired of Ian blushing with nerves, ignoring the matching face of Ethan.

"Club soda, and your time on Friday night?"

Ethan mouthed, 'smooth.'

"I'd happily oblige. I'm Anochi."

"Ian. My sibling over here, will have a tea with lemon. He wouldn't oblige to you spiking it."

'You're good,' Ethan mouthed, adding a wink.

"Sure. I'll get those right away."

"When you say the brothers caused all of this, what do you mean by that?"

Ojeda opened his lips to reply but his lower jaw flopped to the ground.

"Gross!"

"Whoa!"

Randy picked up the lower jaw from the Guide, inspecting it. The forearms surrounding the safe house all migrated towards the collectable piece. They reached in unity, grabbing for the trophy. Chloe helped kick them away as the three went inside.

"One soda. One tea with a lemon twist."

Ethan knew drinks were on the house. Ian was smitten with predisposition.

"You guys know what you want, or do you need a few minutes?"

"I know what I want. It involves more than a few minutes."

The waitress scoffed with embarrassment, though she was flattered.

"I'll surprise you," she intended with double meaning, then making her way to the kitchen.

"My twin, my competitor, how long do you think our game will go on, now that the stakes are raised so high?"

"You want to team up?"

"I have a plan, but I need your help."

"How would we know who wins?"

"Do remember our agreement, prior to the bunker."

"I'd never forget it."

"The day will come, it is approaching. Our escalations will help to multiply how soon."

Ian ran his tongue across his teeth, craving a stick of laced gum. He hadn't considered what his brother was alluding to, if he had, he may not have pulled the press conference stunt.

"What's it like, being another person?"

"Well Randy, that's something you would have to experience for yourself."

"Will you show me where the portal is?"

The blackness hid away Chloe's consideration. Randy assumed wrongly and ignited deliberations.

"You can't just mention it, then hide it away. I'll follow you. I'll stalk you.

You'll go looking for Ian again. When you do, I'll find out.

You won't keep your secret, forever."

"Randy, mellow out. I'll show you."

Randy exhaled his anger.

"Give a girl the decency of response, huh?"

"Sorry. Hey, out of nosiness, what's your name when you travel back?"

"Anochi."

The waitress did in fact surprise the guys, bringing each their favorite appetizers plus main courses.

"Are you a psychic?"

"Nope. There's just something about you, Ian," she flirted.

Ethan gave a thumbs up, his mouth too full for the creation of silent words.

Once the dinner was over, Anochi gave Ian her number.

"I'll be in touch about the business strategy," Ethan reminded, once the flirting session was over with.

"Please do. I'm intrigued."

Chapter 10:
Perceiving A Passerby, Friday Night, The Wager

Ian threw his burner phone in the fountain. Looking at the collection of coins at the bottom, he wondered if there were more of them or more spirits in Second Chance thanks to the brothers' game. Betting on the latter, he flipped in a nickel of his own.

Placing his ball of chewable nicotine in a trashcan, he walked away from the water spout. He liked to walk the city streets. Each one was unique, though most had the same things in common. Neon signs, graffiti, alleys and the homeless were always shared.

He was buying a rival newspaper to read his competitors, when he was tapped on his back.

"Hands o-," he begin to bark, stopping once he saw the face of the tapper.

"I thought that was you!"

"Been a long time, Cassie. Forgive my outburst."

"Is Ethan around somewhere?"

"No."

"Did you guys have a fallout?"

"Nothing like that. I saw him recently actually, but he left on business."

"Too bad. How have you been? Sit, I have time. Reminisce me."

Ian sat down on the bench, forgetting about the paper he had just purchased. He forgot it at the stand and it was resold to another.

"So, how's space?"

"Roomy. How's Earth?"

"Crowded, but thinning always."

"That it is. You know, in all my travels, I really thought I'd find a sign of Chloe."

"Did you ever?"

"No. Nothing. Do you think about her still?"

"Never ends."

Cassandra grew watery eyed, her smile concealing her pain.

"We can change subject," Ian suggested.

Cassie nodded, it was needed.

Leaving the boys behind, Chloe left the safety structure. She skipped over the beating lumps, heading to the portal. Even without guts, she followed her inner instinct. There was something special about the moment in time. Destiny likely.

When she returned into Anochi, she found herself spraying on perfume. Her hair was done, as were her nails. She looked incredible. Then, the doorbell rang. She finished putting in the other earring, then went to see who awaited her.

"Flowers?"

Ian hesitated, not sure why his date looked so astonished. She took them, but remained quiet.

"All okay?"

"Couldn't be better," she managed to confess.

The car ride was a tad less awkward. By the time they reached their date headquarters, Chloe felt congenial. She almost felt envious of Anochi because of the courtesy provided by Ian. He had grown up to be a dignified man. She was very grateful to be with him, even if he was with somebody else.

"This place is tasteful," she admired looking at the extravagant chandeliers.

"Nothing, nobody else here, compares to you, tonight."

If she wasn't already in love with him, she knew that Anochi would be when this night ended. It winced her to think of it ever having to reach a close. She stared through his pupils in to his soul.

"I would rather be nowhere else, with no other."

They examined the glare off the lights dancing in the other's eyes. If Hell had a joke department, this was a pure offshoot. It was love all over again for Ian. For Chloe, a reconnection with her soulmate.

Anochi's spirit woke up in pitch darkness. The walls around her were thundering.

"Where am I?"

Her call out went void of reply.

The rattling all around her started to make her queasy, then legs split to reveal Second Chance. She was grabbed by her throat by a slew of veins. Her spirit was absorbed, feeding the Visculoquists.

Ever drowning, Anochi's spirit was frozen beneath the flow of five water bodies.

Chloe began to choke, then bleed from Anochi's epidermis. She jerked to the floor, pouring red. Once she was in the back of an ambulance, Ian started on his quest to find Ethan. They rushed the bleeding beauty to the hospital. Hope was scarce. His rendezvous was ruined, his date was dead. If she wasn't at demise yet, he figured she was certainly dying. As rage built, so did his desire to craft havoc.

"Come to talk business?"

Ian, who was smoking a cigarette he had bummed, pushed Ethan aside and assaulted the nearest bottle.

"I'm cursed," he sputtered, wasting a portion of his swig.

"Wasn't tonight your outing with that waitress? How did you manage to ruin it?"

"IMBECILE!"

Ian hollered, breaking the glass against his brother's skull. Ethan countered, putting Ian to sleep.

Once Ian gained consciousness, he found himself tied to a chair strapped with explosives.

"Have you regained your marbles, Ian. You left me with no choice."

"She's dying, right now."

"Who? The waitress?"

"Of course, who else?"

"What happened?"

"I'm not sure. She just began to suffocate, then seep blood."

"Truly terrible!"

"Give me a few sticks of gum, I beg of thee."

Ethan fetched without question, giving Ian his fix.

"I need to erase some folks," Ian sloshed through smacks of nicotine saliva.

"You're not in the proper frame of mind."

Ian spat at him, raging.

"Let me get you out of that contraption, then we can get planning."

"I demand a wager."

"Place your bet."

"Two more jobs. Whoever can create the biggest outcry wins. Then, we follow through with our agreement."

"You haven't even heard me out yet. What have you up your sleeve?"

Ian smiled wide, spittle dripping from his mouth like he were a rabid beast.

The twins took turns laying out their plans, both agreeing to the wager once they both put forth their plots. A grand storm was coming, not only from the competing kin, but for the general public, as well as the beyonds.

Chapter 11:

After Hour Visitation, A Realm In Ruin, The Confessional

Ian slipped past the snoozing guard with ease. The nurses proved a little more difficult, but stealth was a part of his expertise.

He held the hand of Anochi, bawling for her survival. The moonlight lit up a part of her bed, but her face remained concealed.

"I would have given my heart to you. I cannot offer my life, as it is within oath, but I would be tempted to cast it away for the feelings you provided me. Life chuckles when symmetry fails. What a callous thing existence is. I deserve to share your hideous termination, yet I exist."

"Close your brutish beliefs," Chloe ridiculed in her own voice.

Ian scooted backwards and fell out of the chair, his tailbone throbbed. He pressed his back against the far wall, panting exhaustively.

"What abyss have I aligned with?"

Ian asserted, immersed in shadow.

"Ian, taste my kiss with yours. Come to me. We have been apart for so long."

Ian squawked with lunacy. Chloe rose, still seeping crimson juice. The moon illuminated her face, causing Ian to claw his cheeks downwardly, streaking grooves that oozed with plasma.

"You bleed the color of rust?"

Ian placed his hands in the narrow beam of light, seeing the outlandish accusation. He dropped to his knees, sniveling.

"You were never alive," Chloe discerned plainly.

Ian sobbed, his tears sizzling when they crossed the open gashes.

Ian's psyche was hardly the only thing in tatters. Ojeda and Randy fled from the flaming safe house, the paths abnormally pulsing. Ojeda lost his footing, glitching out in the blue grass. Forearms enclosed him, peeling him in strips. Randy kept running, his digital friend another figure in his past.

The Frahmasphere lingered just above Randy's head. He could feel its moist contents against his spirit. The usual arrangements of splendid color seemed to fade to gray. Within the flashes of the colorless were Visculoquists!

"I was alive, Ethan was the one born deceased."

"Your organs weren't alive, they were switched out. Donors allowed you a life outside of Second Chance. That's your connection to the realm. Ethan's stillbirth is his. You were miracles. Both of you. Only you two can put an end to the crossover."

"What crossover?"

"The one where Second Chance and Earth merge. It is close, but something is preventing it."

"The competition."

"Dare I ask?"

"You'll find out. When it happens, you, along with the world, will know when it ends."

"You're starting to scare me."

"If you knew my cause, you'd already be scared."

The veins reached then flickered away. Randy ran, desperate to survive. They ripped Spot from his hands, but he just ran quicker. Intestinal tracts slithered through the grass, assisting in the hunt for the runaway.

The realm suddenly turned black, expelling a Visculoquist masqueraded as his mom.

"Quick, follow me!"

"You're not my mother," Randy argued, his ankles getting coiled with guts.

"Randall, it's me," Stacy enticed, taking over his mother's features.

Randy jumped, reaching his hand into the Frahmasphere. A hand grasped his wrist from the other side, then tried to pull him through. A tug of war ensued tearing Randy's spirit in two. His upper half went into the green fog, the bottom stayed behind and turned to rock.

"Ian, I know that you and Ethan are responsible for the future intersecting. Tell me how? Nothing can sway my love for you."

"Your answer will come. Keep an eye on the news. When the third act starts, you'll know it."

Ian kissed the bleeding lips of his first, and only, love. Excusing himself, he stealthily snuck out of the hospital.

"Ian?"

"Ethan, actually. Do you know my brother?"

"From his searching for Chloe."

"Where's the rest of you?"

"Back there," Randy replied, nodding towards the open closet.

"Tough luck there. Keep yourself together. I have a very important letter to write."

Randy ignored the crude innuendo, using his arms for legs. He placed himself in front of the TV, propped himself and watched the coyote with a knack for failed murder attempts. A show he had never seen before, he liked it, but pondered why he had not been aware of it previously.

Ethan sat and wrote out his terminal message.

'My exception, my Cassandra,

I think that by time this writing reaches you, I will have left this world. If not, then my ending will come close after. As I am sure you have heard the news of the latest, most abhorrent, onslaught. I have to remove a burden from my back. I hope you will not call me a monster for what words lay ahead. You have always had my heart, but there's things in which you're unaware.

Many years ago, Ian and I met the remains of our father. He imparted unto us our purpose for existing. One, that if I look back now, I still see without regret. We are in a bleak rivalry, one that was set forth when we were born. We were both handed a second chance, when others usually receive the burnt end. We were given the miraculous. Our survivals set forth a reflective realm.

Truth be transparent, I must confess that the shedding of lives making global attention, we are responsible for. My brother and I. Fret not, for their lives continue in a dinension of artistry. A 4-D world, where the children can grow up and continue their lives. Tragedy is biased. I would call our work, subjective serendipity. One may label them victims, but to us, our clients are given the gift of opportunity. One that we share with them, a second life. We should be revered as prodigies, but they will surely put us in the books as villains. That is, if we even make the history texts at all...

In another life, I would have chose a road that led to some form of an us. Love me as I am, for I am guilty of nothing. I feel nothing to beg forgiveness for. Our work is nearing completion. One left, then we will bid a good riddance.

Farewell, the one who was yours,

Ethan.'

Chapter 12:
Ethan's Game

The day had arrived. Big bellied friends stood in a line, body paint across their nude torsos repping the team they were rooting for. A clash of the biggest idols who wore helmets and tights. Hot dogs and beer sold at twice their value. The crowds roared mindlessly, waiting for the kick that would begin the end. The final pigskin contest of the season, which many find their meaning in.

The score was close throughout the entire length of the four quarters. Drunken fans hurled insults at the fans of their opponents, while whistles blew on the field.

The match went into overtime. Whoever won next, would gain the trophy. Gamblers did their bidding on their teams' odds. The thousands of mouths sat hushed when the ball was hiked. Once the passer had possession, the pig flesh burst with projectiles. Glass shards, nails and other severing types of shrapnel hit the players of both teams. Any survivors would never compete again. Then, a few helmets burst with flames. Mouth guards merged lips permanently as craniums crisped. Once the fans saw their icons fall, a mass delirium settled in. Fans began to throw punches, stomps and headbutts. A sick cycle of battery developed from the work of the twins.

The ones not brawling set off to the parking lot, retreating. Ian sat in wait. More bombs of armory continued to detonate behind them, while their cerebrums were blown out their occiputs. Cars started, but were exploded upon ignition. Ian aimed for major arteries.

The stadium erupted with a mighty boom, showering the parking lot with detritus and anatomy chunks.

Lights strobed, blending in the sparks from Ian's barrel. Shot after shot was fired, eliminating any living escapees. When none were with breath, Ian packed it up and headed to Ethan's location.

"Game over," Ian divulged.

"Theirs of course."

"Goes without saying."

"Did you tell Chloe?"

"I hinted. She knows now, or will soon."

"I confessed to Cassie."

"Penned?"

"Naturally."

"Could be a delay in the closer."

"Why would you speak that?"

"Society is going to tear themselves to shreds."

"Won't they intervene?"

"A proper foreshadowing, I would infer."

An outpouring of chaotic events filled the streets. The two biggest teams, bearing the most popular names, were gone. Dead, along with the final say. Who won? The siblings. Nobody else. The void of a score settlement meant Hell to pay.

Skyscrapers that were ablaze, blocked out the day with clouds of dark smoke. The streets ran with the blood of battered citizens. Corpse clutter became a common sighting. Police units disbanded, unable to protect or serve, a lot of them chipping in with the vicious reaction. Anarchy reigned for a time as the savageness escalated.

Molotov cocktails burned down homes, precincts, jobs, daycares, you name it, it was aflame. Some sport fanatics willingly stood in the fires, preferring to melt over the constant wondering of the final score.

Chloe watched the television in disbelief. The level of commitment was unsurpassed. She knew Ian had something big planned, but this was behemoth in capacity. She fled the hospital since it was slowly withering to ash.

What was once a simple walk, now was a road to destruction. Cars were dented, fleeting to embers. Some of the charred vehicles had occupants, most self sacrificial, some not.

Chloe wanted to hate Ian for causing the apocalyptic reality, but she couldn't. A piece of her wished to congratulate him and Ethan. The planning, the effort. She had to grant credit to whom it was due, her childhood friends certainly were worthy of goal fulfillment. The world was theirs, but they were about to face a new adversary. This fresh opponent intended to take the reign. He was coming with a militia of organs.

Norval's ship flowed aligned with the downstream tubes of digestion towards a meeting of five waterfalls. When he hit the bottom, the limbed boat shattered, resulting in his soul slipping through a dimensional layer, entering the domain of The Aboriginables.

The ground and sky were made up of foil. His steps echoed, reflecting off the silver base. His presence would be noticed, so he decided to draw immediate attention.

"COME OUT! MAKE YOURSELVES KNOWN!"

His vocals bounced off the tin floor, acoustically resonating from the crumpled heavens.

'Nice try. We don't come out when the Interval is upon,' watery DNA scribbled.

He didn't have a spare second, before the aluminum stage tore apart, releasing a mastodon twice as ginormous as the first. The Matriarch was composed of human bones, mountains of them! Covering the skeletal structure were plates of metal armor, remnants of combat. Out of the bones, tusks of marrow splintered away in opposing direction, covering the surface of the osseous Queen.

Far off, Portiis could make out the sound of edges sharpening, prepping for dominance.

Norval darted his eyes around, then he spotted a well. He ran to it then dove into the vapor, leaving the brawling to the bygones.

Chapter 13:
Integration Of Second Chance

The sun eclipsed, shrouding the Earth in shade. The green grass turned blue, the blue sky turned green. Pavements became infused with cardiac muscles. All the rocks and mountains changed to a hue of orange. Trees were replaced with conjoined lower limbs, while flowers evolved to upper ones. The waters switched to pink in pigmentation, swimming with entrails. From the waters, colossal rooks arose, embedded with the faces of all those who passed through Second Chance. The planet illuminated, the light flowing up and expanding rather than down then out. Structures now looked digitalized, their outlines protruding from their natural tones.

Unlike their predecessors, the forelimbed trees weren't stationary. They trampled through the lands, stepping on people scaled to insect. The forearms retrieved the smooshed souls, placing them within the rooks.

The rooks were also mobile, taking position of the major monuments of Earth. They made suffocating sounds across the planet surface, as if they were still drowning beneath meeting waters. They opened simultaneously once positioned, conceiving the Visculoquists. Only here, their veins were behind them making them look enslaved. The rest of their headless abdomens were still decorated with internal organs, their insides hollow.

Time froze. Cassandra put the letter aside and got out her telescope. She had expected an arrival, but not so soon. She didn't own a TV, so she was clueless to the things occurring post Ethan's round. She preferred to lose herself in written word. She wanted to explore outside her world, what was in it was obsolete.

The spaceship landed in her yard. It resembled a sideways, revolving hourglass. The silver bars of the ship remained in constant motion, even when it was in an immovable state. The glass opened, letting out two drivers instead of spilling time measurement sand.

The drivers were identical. They wore suits of eyes that were sewed on, making them literal battle vests. The eyes would blink here and there, presumably still living. The drivers' outlines looked as if they were created from aqua. Their cyan skin crawled with shifting tentacles and crashing waves. They spoke through clicks. Their typewriter voices created plain text in the air before them. Essentially they were double captioned, typing the same words at the same time.

'Greetings Greetings, Cassandra Cassandra.'

"What brings you all so far? We weren't schedule to meet, yet."

'Look look around around, your your planet planet is is under under invasion invasion.'

"From who?"

'The the demon demon of of the the Frahmasphere Frahmasphere.'

"Can you stop it?"

They nodded in unison.

"How soon?"

'First first we we must must study study, but but it it will will be be a a precise precise victory victory.'

"Help us, please. Hasten it!"

'You you have have our our word word.'

From the center of the eyes on their uniforms, a black hole expanded outward erasing their location. Their ship remained in her yard, still in rotation.

Chloe knocked on the hotel room door, Ethan answered.

"Long time," he stated, looking over the woman she had came to be.

"Where's Ian?"

"Around. Come in."

"I come bearing urgency."

"What?"

"They're here."

"Who?"

"The pawns."

Ethan scratched his chin, moistening his lips with his tongue.

"You told us time wasn't of essence."

"It wasn't.

When was the last time that you two went outside?"

"Why?"

Ian interrupted, including himself to the discussion.

"Second Chance is now Earth. Earth is now Second Chance."

"Our work isn't finished."

"He's premature."

"Who?"

"Your father."

The Frahmasphere split to the west. Riding on a chariot of moth winged lungs was the one with the halo of blades. One hand held the reins to the Visculoquists, his other held chains that led to each of the rooks. His holey sternum suckled, each bullet hole a little mouth of despair. He cracked his neck causing the knives to plunge in then out.

The hands all turned his direction with honor, maybe servitude. The slithering guts as well. They erected their slinky bodies like a ready to strike cobra.

"Let us eradicate the rest," the twins' dad reverberated, the echoes travelling down the links to his army.

The vaporous sky sealed again, a staple in the conquering.

"What's his goal?"

"Defeat the Spacemen, same as you two."

"How did you figure all this out?"

"I glimpsed the future."

"What's to come?"

"A flood, the Earth kind. If you two don't get your mission complete before he does, this grotesque hybrid of Hell and Second Chance is permanent. Due to the insane backlash from phase three, he thought you were complete. He came to establish dominance. Prove him wrong, he loses. The Spacemen will then flood our planet, assuming that last detail. All I know is this planet ends in water."

Chapter 14:
The Interdimensional Battle The Cosmic

The Spacemen returned to their ship without bothering to fill in Cassandra. They made no hesitation with lifting into the green misty sky. Whatever their rush was, Cassie knew that time was definitely of the essence.

"They're gone," Chloe revealed, no long channeling her sister's sight.

"To run from the fight?"

"Gathering the troops."

"Noble."

The Spacemen came alone on their next trip out.

"What's the deal?"

'We we came came to to tell tell you you to to take take cover cover.'

"Reinforcements? When?"

'Day day proceeding proceeding tomorrow tomorrow, Earth Earth time time.'

"Will anyone survive?"

'We we recommend recommend you you to to take take shelter shelter.'

"We missed our shot," Ethan snarled, looking up at the tipped over hourglass fleet in the air above.

"Let them war it out. We take the winner," Ian steered his sibling with verbal correction.

"Chloe, can you take control of your sister?"

"I didn't expect you to be the one to ask, Ethan, but yes. Will I betray my sister?"

She looked to Ian, her heart picking up a steadier beat somewhere in some road in Second Chance.

"I love my sister deeply, but Ian has always held my heart."

"Then, I shall reroute my initial sequence. We will be prepped to challenge the dominant force," Ian signified.

The legged trees burst with varicose veins, setting forth a flock of skeletal owls. The swirling rims of the hourglasses began to spin faster than the speed of sight. Shooting the owls with water based lasers. The flying time keepers fought against the Visculoquists at ground level too. Blasting apart their organ skin tags, enraging the dad of the brothers.

The veins and chains were unleashed. The rooks teamed up with the varicose trees, returning the attack on the soldiers from the cosmos. They fought with brute force, while the Visculoquists used the art of lassoing. Ships exploded, organs and limbs were liquefied.

Chloe watched through her sister's retinas. The scenery was so brilliant in tint, but so terrible in what unfolded within it. She was glimpsing but a fraction, this battle was across all the lands of the planet.

The owls pecked into the ships, eating the tentacled pilots. They were a larger threat than the Visculoquist lassoers. The focus was on the owls' demise, which enabled the drowning rooks and the fused pillars of legs to obtain an offensive advantage for a limited moment.

The ships managed to make a comeback, blasting away the pillars with ease once the hordes of bony birds stopped.

'Surrender surrender,' the lead ship wrote out.

Their demand made the father of the miracle bros snicker. His chest inhaled, absorbing the remnants of the fallen. The blades dug into the noggin of the demon, whose head grew until it broke off of his inwardly sucking upper body. The organs stuck together, crafting an elongated throat. Once the organ scaled body snapped onto the pointy ends hanging out of the severed head, the slithery neck with anatomy moles went up into the atmospheric portal.

The air force kept themselves suspended. Hovering, awaiting the next assault. From where it could come was something that they were unclear about. Their enemy had ascended, so they maneuvered low without limiting their defense to surface only. They stayed alert. Ready to defend mankind's habitat.

For days they waited, but the sky didn't pose a threat. Four weeks passed, then they declared themselves victorious. They landed all around Cassie's dwelling, for she was their trusted contact.

"The Earthlings wish to celebrate," Chloe deceived through her sibling.

'We we would would be be honored honored.'

"Leave your ships, we must go to where they are."

Ian puppeteered the Visculoquists' torsos to give them the personalities and looks of Earth's leaders. With the organs not on the outside, the deceit was simple. He was able to command them by slicing holes in himself, exposing his own organs. He was their father. They were reflections of his survival. His insides being exploited allotted their full control.

The fake ambassadors adored their heroes. The pilots were moved by the magnitude of the ceremony. They were crowned as the defenders of the third. They had misjudged humans. They expected to be snubbed, but instead they teetered worship. Their endeavor praised.

'Thank thank you you. Our our pleasure pleasure.'

They were welcomed to return whenever they would like. A treaty between the Earthlings and the Cosmos was drawn up. The frauds signed in red, using their veins as pens. The Spacemen autographed the air, unable to figure out penmanship. Earth was saved thanks to these strangers from the stars.

Chapter 15:

Ian's Game, Pact Fulfillment

Accompanied by only the dictated Cassandra, the Spacemen made their way to their ships to prepare for departure.

When they were at a certain altitude, their ships went down from small explosions. Every ship was rigged. Some of the pilots fell out, resulting in being crushed by their own crafts. A few survived the crash landings. Ian smacked his lips with a wad of gum, following each down to ensure no survival.

'Help help, we we are are injured injured.'

Bullets cut through the water bodies and then leaked out grains of sand. The tentacles tried to repair the tiny craters, but were taken out with further gunshots.

Chloe's words zigzagged in Ian's focused patience, but he was still a sure shot.

'Save save us us.'

"You too have glimpsed the future," Chloe's voice ricocheted in his thoughts.

Chloe let go of her sister as the shot rang out. Cassie screamed, figuring this must all be a putrid dream. Surely, nobody was this wicked. Why? Who? She asked the questions inside but she already knew the answer. A written confession had informed her. She stopped yelling protests, only long enough to empty her stomach. The brothers' action made her sick.

'Cassandra Cassandra why why?'

"The cartoons we used to watch at your house, they don't exist yet. Presents for the sons of a demon. The demon who desires the finale of the Earth. He had your lives planned out long before your conceptions," Chloe reminded Ian through a tide of memory waves.

'We we are are the the last last of of our our kind kind.'

Several hills of sand was all that remained once Ian picked their race clean. He felt a morsel of remorse for the genocide, but it was the finish to the twins' predetermined objective.

"The characters were supposed to help you both along in your interests. Gifts of influence," the last wave of recall told Ian.

Their dad fell from the Frahmasphere, writhing in excruciation like a slug covered in salt. His pride was his downfall. Had he let his boys execute the Spacemen, then invaded, he would have won. Seeing the future, didn't mean he could jumpstart doomsday. His sons were a step ahead thanks to their slaying of the Starmen. A surge of vendetta spiked throughout his veins.

The world, or what was left of the human race, mourned the loss of their guardians. They wanted justice to be served upon whoever had taken the warriors out. The crime was inexcusable, almost as absurd as the sport stars' slaughter, but the true heroes weren't idolized and likely were only appreciated for the time being. All over the surface of the third, silence befell in memoriam.

"It has been a journey," Ethan smiled, extending his hand out.

Ian took it. He was strapped in proximity mines.

His brother was in a compact set of walls with just enough room for him to stand up straight. The sniper rifle that Ian always used, was positioned at the top of the confinement. The structure was built to allow the bullet to bounce back and forth, all the down, ripping holes in the recipient.

"I won?"

"A tie," Ethan remedied.

Ian nodded to approve. He let go of his twin's hand then walked across the auditorium, mounting himself on a rigged exercise bike. They had made this pact when they first discovered the bunker. A promise of their own executions. Each dying by the brand of the other.

Chloe stood nearby waiting for her moment. When it came, she pushed the detonation button without care. Ian peddled, his brother watching and readying himself for implementation. The initial blast took Ian's calves, he kept trying to peddle using only his thighs.

Ian was incinerated instantly after the second explosion. Ethan died almost as quick, dripping rust that is eternal. The sides of his anatomy dressed in holes. His internal parts penetrated thoroughly. The game was over.

Chloe unfastened the rifle, taking it with her.

Cassie was trying to locate her phone when the first bullet pierced her cheek. Another took her right kneecap. Both shots managed to hit major blood vessels, causing her to bleed out.

With her sister taken out by her hands, Chloe set fire to the letters from Ethan exonerating the persons responsible for the years of domestic terrorism.

"Th-th-th-that's all folks," she chuckled to herself, imitating her favorite character that she used to visit the brothers' house to watch.

Slinging the murder weapon over her left shoulder, Chloe decided to carry on the work of the siblings. The seeping of blood through her skin never stopped, but never ran dry. An infinite curse on her, one that mirrored her betrayals.

The 4-D effects of Second Chance glitched away, returning the Earth back to normal. The vibrance vanished, so did the rooks, the trees of limbs, Visculoquists and all other traces of the crossover. The slate would wipe itself clean, becoming nothing more than a harrowing dream. Time would forget the twins' competitive ventures.

Society tried to rebuild, leaving their accounts of terror unspoken and unwritten. What they refused to forgive was never knowing who won the ballgame that season. The sensation that the inconclusive wound left would not ever recover. To the scorned sports fans, healing from that disaster wasn't one they could permit. Over a hundred homicides happened over disputes speculating the game's results. Those imprisoned over score arguments had to be separated from the other inmates who were fans of the opposite team. The rivalry was reminiscent of a certain set of brothers. One of many reflections of their work.

Chapter 16:
Chloe's Crusade

Lovers skated in heart shaped patterns. They held hands through fuzzy gloves. Infatuation spread over their expressions with toothy smiles. Young passion, often fleeting, was coursing the lines of blood throughout the couple's mainframes.

"The icicles glistening on the leaves cannot dare to reflect the beauty in your eyes."

"You're just too sweet."

Cheeks blushed, ticking beats fluttered within chests and skates made little grooves in ice.

"In the name of true love," Chloe snarled.

The girl's eye blasted out of its socket, as the two were creating a figure eight on the rink. The boy's bellybutton received a bullet, sending him to the icy ground. The girl tumbled her way to where he dropped. He garbled blood, his girlfriend kneeling over him gripping his convulsing hand. The side of her temple then burst with silver and she fell on top of her boyfriend, who was still twitching in agony. Neither died suddenly nor lived.

Others were shot too. She wasn't aiming to execute, she was pointing the barrel at non lethal areas so that her victims would endure slow demise.

"You'll thrive in Second Chance," Chloe assured from afar.

The trigger was pulled two dozen times more, then she fled the scene.

Horns blared, brakes were pumped, as the traffic piled into a cluster of unmoving metal. The construction was pushing the row of commuters into a single lane. Blinkers were turned on with gestures of attitude. Frustration gave way to fright when windshields were fired into, blasting the brains of their occupiers.

Chloe grinned once the jammed drivers and construction workers no longer squirmed. Kids with backpacks, men with briefcases, women with perms, none were spared. All were fired on indiscriminately. Ian would be proud. Her shots were accurate for what their purpose was. She felt exuberant dealing death. Both of her temples were fused with the minds of the brothers, one attached to each side. They were held by a bracketed container, preserved, feeding into Chloe's thoughts. Their expertise was now her's to wield. The mission was the same, to send people to a better place, one named Second Chance.

When the brothers were shaking hands, the tops of their skulls were exposed. While they awaited their demise, a repurposed claw machine arm removed their thought processors via a series of laser splices. The organs were collected, then an IED blew away any clues that remained. Marked as dead years prior, Chloe knew her identity would remain enigmatic.

She wasn't the only one wrecking peace, the violence would never cease on the lands of Earth. Most committed theirs with no happy agenda.

Eyes twinkled as two studied the features of the other. The gentleman took his best friend for two and a half years by her hand.

"You are my everything. My world revolves around you and only you. To always keep that in your mind, I offer a revolving circle to you. Will you marry me?"

"I do," Chloe mimicked, her lips matching the fiancee's.

Then, the ring flung embers of extreme heat, melting the faces of the newly engaged. Two became one as their skin fused to a mess of flesh.

There was a device left to Cassie. A miniature wheel wired to a triggering mechanism. Ethan had intended for his soulmate to answer the call to arms. It was never imagined that Chloe could be the one capable of carrying on the cause. She clutched the ignition system to her organless sternum. For the first time ever she longed for children. Barren, she spoke the phrase to herself, turning the wheel that was connected to all the major monuments on all continents.

"Look, fireworks!"

The major structures erupted with fire, creating a globally shared sense of hopelessness. The sorrow, drove many to take their own existences away. They weren't expecting to be reborn but they would be, just like the ones before them.

On the anniversary of the battle of the non Earthers, there was held a private ceremony. Leaders from every country attended and paid their respects to the star saviors.

When the moment of silence was to occur, massive booms filled its spot, massacring the remembrance. All countries locked down, public events cancelled. Traveling banned. Nowhere was safe, nobody was without a target on them. Hermitage reigned in the nerves of mankind. Neighbors grew estranged, as did families.

Chloe began to learn the ways of the blade. Specializing in sharpened edges for collecting of organs. She sewed them into mannequins, forming a race of Visculoquist slaves.

She was watching the evolution of technology, capitalizing on its outburst in the public home. She brought the brand, Coyote J., to life. Costs were low, quality didn't suffer. Her company became a household name. The stocks skyrocketed, making Chloe a millionaire. She had to assume the identity of Anochi, since she and her sibling were legally dead. All of her brand's electronics were bombs. Some filled with crude projectiles, others were block leveling blasts. When they were set off, she was sitting in the middle of her factory. Surrounded by immanent destruction, she was vaporized, as were the newly built Visculoquists, along with half of the planet!

The world shaking detonations, were simultaneous with a series of natural disasters. Somewhere in China, a little girl had monsters made from a peculiar type of paper. Her accidents would drown the Earth, turning it back to water.

Chapter 17:
Renewable Continuation

On the eight day, God found the Earth as He had left it. Pocket cells of His repurposed wrath left residual footprints that would transpire events of mass violence in the second Earth. All things have the quality of reflection. The same timers had infected the planet to become a product of interdimensional bloodshed.

Second Chance became renewed. Now hailing as, Third Beginnings, it serves a hybrid of the first Earth and the one that was being born after Chloe's combustion. It has crossover glitches in the new era, some would refer to it as The Mandela Effect. None are wrong due to the coexistences. The combinations weren't limited in their reaches. Different folks can easily experience things in the other realms. The dimensional bleeding is a major factor in the traumatic ongoings on the second form of Earth. It is commonplace that every untimely occurrence is a simple trickling of echoes from the first world. There were many dormant demons during the first intersection, their reflections are the root of the continual upheavals.

When a great war waged in Heaven, Third Beginnings was a forgotten kingdom. An apple bred Hell opening it into an abyss for an arrogant angel and his disciples. Down within Hell's caverns, slithers the blade adorned, organ bodied, serpent. Ruler of Hades, it swims the Lake of Fire, miles of intestines flow behind it appearing as its progeny.

Third Beginnings was a plain void of despair. It looked more digital than ever before, its colors brilliant, almost cartoonish. Tears, are a term unheard, as are disease, blood, death, other criminal actions. In their pursuits of subjective serendipity, Ian and Ethan gave meaning to trauma.

Randy found his way back to Spot. His mother smiled, wearing a turned over fish bowl full of water on her cranium, her lungs expelling liquid continuously. The young man with a plush cow for a bestie was not given an opinion from anybody. Things were welcomed rather than shunned. Discrimination, the residents know not what that means.

Red rose fields provided nectar to butterflies with lungs for wings. The sky was the shade of salmon, with guts for clouds, a mirrored image of the chemical trails of second Earth. The trees were stone pillars of Ethan and Ian, whom without, none of this would be reality; who would be cursed in the second incarnation, rebuilding and inseparable, always teething, eternal. Water runs aqua in pigment like the epidermis of the deleted aeronauts. Within the clashing falls there is rumored to be seen octopi with human hearts. Their sands are said to walk with shrimp that carry hourglass shells.

Stacy and Hannah, each got a clone of their muscular stud. They go out for fries and ice cream every Friday.

Stacy patted the head of the Pookins, who purred at her ankles. She had somehow retained his memory, some believe it was an imprint of unconditional love.

Chloe was never thought of again, her work insignificant. All she had done was practice sadism, simply put.

Cassandra was reincarnated as retinas, given a new name, body and purpose; Geneva Shaw. A choice she would beg to take back, but one that she was forced to cope with. Her avenging her unfairness resulted in an extension of torment. Her outcome, had she chosen forgiveness, would have been beautiful.

The twins' mother was offered a third redemption, but she declined. She didn't trust the infinite, not after the last two. Rightfully so, she became a planet, one unoccupied, galaxies away from Earth and its innumerous dimensions.

Ojeda forever was silent, from his own mouth at least, given the gift of Ventriloquism. He had two dummies, Mr. And Mrs. Nusam. They were a chipper, helpful duo, the polar difference of their original embodiments.

Tag, was the running game in Third Beginnings. Randy had begun the trend, which grew to be a favorite fast. He gave his mom Spot, then hollered, "I'm it," to a group of kids. They laughed, then shrieked in a fun manner, as Randy grew organs on the outside of his spirit. His head snapped off, closing his eyes so he could not to peek. He counted down from ten, then the vein limbed Visculoquist started searching for the hid away children. The players had to mind their wits, for the hunter could take any form to try to cloak itself as a familiar. If it wrapped you up, you were the new predator, taking on its repulsive form. The game went on indefinitely. There were always willing participants, several were enthused to take on the role of pursuant, taking solace in donning themselves the antagonist.

Swimming was another popular activity. Sightings of the tentacled hearts were a rarity, but swimming beside captioned fish with eyeball scales was a regular thing. Teenagers typically snuck down to the meeting of the falls, they played chess with soul remnants. The pebbles were imprints of spirits in despair. Similar to how Gray World spillovers would commonly be mislabeled as hauntings in the second Earth.

There was a petting Zoo, but the animals were constructed of forearms and forelegs. They were tame, no call for feeding, easily maintained. They existed for the enjoyment of the Zoo's visitors.

Ojeda would often guide tours, his puppets in charge of the narration. Nobody found the exhibit creepy, for that would be a concept unknown to Third Beginners.

Some goers adopted the appendage beasts as pets, taking their beloved phantoms for walks one a day. Some taught the limbed creatures tricks, spawning an annual contest.

The yellow rocks and caves harbor orange and pink owls carved from padparadscha. They have perfect pitch melodies that are sung from two sets of beaks.

Often times, without a hint of the onset, a green fog fills Third Beginnings. It, is a vapor portal to the Gray World, when it settles there is a season of sorrow. During these times, hermitage is advised. Those who ignore the advisement undergo drowning in a purple flood, while they suffocate they also relive the abhorrent events of the brothers. The season of the Frahmasphere is momentary, it comes and goes like storms.

Other brave souls are taken to a purgatory during these seasons. There, they are forced to participate in *The Event*. Unlike the spirits from the other realms, they cannot successfully complete the game. All that they experience is the stabbings per their failing. These flashes of netherworlds are brief, like peeping through a falling keyhole. When they're gone, the euphoria recycles and all is as it should be.

There is also a season where the sky pours snowflakes of blood. The red particles are warm to the touch. Square bloodmen are built by the kids there. Depending on air quality, the snow army can appear silver. It isn't harmful to the souls upon handling, but some found out that digestion was poisonous. It was only during the first bloodletting snowfall that taste was a temptation. Being new, it wasn't yet discovered as DNA drops. Once the spirits developed sores that burst, mites formed that then fed on the open lesions. The eating of the sores leads to irreversible lacerations. Not many tasted of the metallic liquid after hearing the fine details of those stories.

The light still shines upwards, radiating from glass organs. The bejeweled viscus parts project brilliant illumination. The Third Beginners have no concept of night. There are times of serenity, and periods of persecution, just another parallel mirror to the complexion of Earth, phase one and the currents.

Portiis fell through the Frahmasphere for a prolonged time. When he was given a destination, he found himself merged with Third Beginnings. Unfortunately, he was given an altered version of the paradise. His new land was ruled by pachyderms assembled from human skulls, complete with the scalps.

The trees that feed the anatomical mammals were Aboriginable, who shaved off flakes of rust for the animals with human hides.

Norval slashed his wrists, longwise, assuming guaranteed euthanasia. When he bled copper, he knew something was terribly awry. The atmosphere turned to fire, spilling over the snake of the burning lake, the one with scales of human internals. The knives were still inlayed in the beasts' cranium, the handles filleted and absent. The tongue flickered and was forked.

Norval's spirit tore from within with crude jags of sharpened points. They decorated him head to foot, no less agonizing than they would have been had he still been alive. He grew as tall as the shiny edged trees, losing all memory of who he was, or what he once might have been. Now, he was Norviis The Tiller, the one with a garden to fill. He looked at the functioning scutes lining the monstrous in length ventral tube body, eyeing his crop. From the organ tags, Norviis The Aboriginable would harvest his own race of steel. Robotic Visculoquists who would help manipulate the second and third Earth. They run off a wet electric and settled as soil. Sour and infecting.

When a lightning fell from Heaven, taking his devotees with him, a deformed soul, quilled with vortexes of points scraped along the mesh between him and the Earth trying to thin the veil. The Tiller has been scraping ever since. Norviis starves in the meantime, needing nourishment, his scuffing perpetual.

As you find yourself reading about him, he can smell your inner thoughts. Sit long enough, very silently, you may even feel him taste your mind. If so, hold your breath, maybe you can hear his boundless abrading! If you can, then this truly is a story's end.

Those who did not, be advised, for he is already sniffing your scent, tracking down your cerebral nutrients. For you, this is the climax, not yet the conclusion.

Don't miss out!

Visit the website below and you can sign up to receive emails whenever Christopher Besonen publishes a new book. There's no charge and no obligation.

https://books2read.com/r/B-A-NQAP-STGUB

BOOKS 2 READ

Connecting independent readers to independent writers.